Gospel End

ROB FROST

MINSTREL
Eastbourne

Front cover design by Vic Mitchell

British Library Cataloguing in Publication Data

Frost, Rob
    Gospel end.
    I Title
    823.914 [F]
    ISBN 1-85424-161-3

Printed in Great Britain for
Minstrel, an imprint of Monarch Publications Ltd
1 St Anne's Road, Eastbourne, E Sussex BN21 3UN by
Made and printed in Great Britain by
BPCC Hazell Books
Aylesbury, Bucks, England
Member of BPCC Ltd.
Typeset by Watermark, Crostwight, Norfolk.

**To Andrew and Chris
and the upcoming generation**

With special thanks to my wife, Jacqui, and my friends Richard and Meryl Smith who read the manuscript as it appeared week by week, who lived with me in the imaginary world of Gospel End and whose advice was invaluable!

Thanks also to Steve Deal of Stripes Theatre Company and Marian Arthur for help with co-ordination of the allied 'Gospel End' stage play and tour. I'm also grateful to publisher Tony Collins for suggesting the concept of a novel.

Gospel End

This is the story of a tightly knit group of people who are enveloped by the traditional chapel culture which they've known all their lives. Slowly but surely the chapel, and the culture associated with it, is destroyed. It is an unnerving and threatening experience. Finally, the chapel closes, and it seems that all they've been working for has gone for ever.

The new minister, Geoffrey Notes, struggles to find the way ahead for the church, and his role within it – and the battles he has to fight highlight many of the issues which overwhelm young Christians today.

The death of the chapel culture, however, is the key to the future. Through the trauma of losing everything which is so precious to them the people rediscover their purpose.

The story is a parable of what could happen in Britain today.

Chapter One

High Hopes

At precisely midday on Friday morning the theological college principal entered the seminar room with the news they were all waiting for. He peered over his half-rimmed spectacles at the twelve young hopefuls who were seated in front of him and smiled a wry smile. He clearly remembered this event in his own life, some forty years before.

'Well, the big moment has come. Your four years of hard labour in this hallowed place are nearly over and I have now received the details of your first appointment. I know that this is an important moment for you, and I hope you'll remember that the stationing committee has done its best to...'

'Come on, sir, don't keep us in suspense ... let's have it,' said twenty-seven-year-old Geoffrey Notes, who was leaning back in his chair with his hands behind his head, looking confident.

The principal smiled his wry smile again, lifted his clip-board, and began to read. They listened eagerly, because the information he shared would chart the future course of their lives. He deliberately saved the details regarding Geoffrey Notes until last.

'...And for you, Mr Notes, the stationing committee really has excelled itself. You are to begin your ministry in a small rural town called Gospel End, in the Yorkshire Metropolitan area of Great Orton, where an enthusiastic and supportive membership eagerly awaits you.'

The college principal rose immediately, scraping his wooden chair on the floor, and strode out. He had no wish to enter into any discussion with his twelve students.

None of the students moved, but the moment the principal left the atmosphere relaxed.

'Thanks for nothing,' moaned Geoff Notes. 'Isn't it typical? I ask for London suburbia, and I get a small rural town in Yorkshire which no one's ever heard of.'

'You think you've got problems?' smiled Janet Winter, a petite thirty-year-old with sparkling eyes and an infectious giggle. 'I asked for overseas ... and I got Shetland.' Everyone laughed; they had been waiting for this announcement for months and their laughter was a release of tension.

'That just about sums it up,' Geoff sighed. 'They didn't really listen to us at those interviews at all ... they're using us to fill the spaces where no one else wants to go. I've never lived in a rural town like Gospel End in my life. I don't think I could survive in a place like that – what do they really know about me?'

Janet Winter had stopped giggling. She knew that Geoff wasn't joking and she could see that he was really upset. To her, it mattered little whether she was being sent to the Caribbean or Malaysia, Kenya or Shetland, and her commitment to Christ was unshakeable. 'Don't take the news personally, Geoff. The stationing committee isn't trying to get at you ... in the end you have to believe that God's behind it all.'

'Janet, must you be pious *all* the time? Can't you give it a rest? It's such a bore.' Geoffrey Notes stood up and stretched to his full height of six feet two. Little Janet Winter, who was still seated, felt dwarfed by him.

For a moment, an awkward silence filled the air – and then the students began to disperse to the loud noise of scraping chairs. Geoff Notes adjourned to the students' common room and to his favourite poison, a strong black coffee. The dart board was free, so he removed three darts from a small black case in his jacket pocket, took careful aim, and threw the first dart with deadly accuracy.

The game of darts was a form of security for Geoff Notes. He had been playing darts regularly since the age of eleven, and he'd always found that the game helped him to relax when things were worrying him.

He'd learned how to play darts at the inner London youth club run by the local Methodists. The church hall was a dump, and the equipment provided was pathetic, but he and about a dozen of his friends never missed a Friday meeting. It was much preferable to the park shelter where they met on other evenings of the week.

Many of Geoff's middle-class college peers considered his upbringing as 'deprived', but he never saw it as such. The two-bedroom council flat which was home to him, his parents, and his two older brothers, did lack many of the luxuries of more middle-class accommodation ... but there was a life and reality about their family relationships which he felt was second to none. Perhaps, he'd often mused, these middle-class students were the ones who were really deprived.

As Geoff took aim and squinted at the board he pictured the dart board in the old church hall in London where his links with the church had first been forged. George, the fifty-year-old bank manager who ran the club, had first taught him how to play darts ... but he'd also taught him about life and about faith.

It was a church which was committed to caring and to serving; but it wasn't a church with a very lively prayer or worship life and Geoff's understanding of the Bible had never much progressed beyond the children's story-book stage. But, through it all, he had developed a real faith. And because the church had committed itself to 'mission alongside the poor', his call to the ministry was recognised, and the church put considerable resources into educating him at theological college.

Sadly, his grooming for the ministry had created a gulf between him and his family, and as each year of the course went by he visited them less and less. To them he had not only become a Christian – he'd become middle class, and although they were proud of his achievement, they no longer really understood him.

Several others were also in the students' common room making coffee and chatting excitedly about their appointments. There was an atmosphere of mutual support and care, and everyone was saying good things about everyone else's appointment. Geoff continued to throw, but all the time he was listening.

'Barnsley's not too bad ... it's got quite a good football team, and they've got a great swimming pool ...'

'Yes, but the good thing about Brixton is that you're so close to theatre-land ... and there's a very rich cultural mix there. You'll enjoy it.'

'I've heard good reports about the church you're going to in Truro ... they've got a great youth work there. A lot of life...'

Janet Winter was genuinely concerned about Geoff. She'd known him throughout his college training, and been a friend to his wife, Sarah, from the earliest days of her introduction to the college community. She knew how important it was to him to be stationed in London, the city he knew and loved. She also knew that Sarah would be devastated.

Janet left the babble of excited voices and stood watching Geoff. 'You're playing well.'

'Well, if four years in this place has taught me

anything, it's taught me how to play darts.' He threw again.

'I'm sorry if I sounded pious earlier on. You must be very disappointed.' She was genuine in her sentiments.

'All my life I've lived in London, my family are there ... my friends are there ... Sarah's there. Living in Bristol has been hard enough, but Gospel End? It might as well be on the moon.' He took aim and threw another dart, missing the triple. Pulling it abruptly from the board, he continued: 'Besides, you know that Sarah needs to live in London to make the right career moves – unless there happens to be umpteen book publishers in this obscure Yorkshire village in the middle of nowhere.' He sounded less heated, more philosophical.

Geoff's two-year marriage to Sarah had not been easy. She was a career girl, a desk editor in a large London publishing house. Each weekend she made the long pilgrimage to Bristol to be with her husband, and early every Monday morning she braved the jammed M4 to drive back home again. Geoff's preaching engagements near the college prohibited him from sharing the ordeal and visiting her in London.

They had first met during a university rag week in Bristol. She was in her second year, and he in his first. They'd both been recruited to help push a hospital bed around the city's inner ring road to help raise money for a new children's ward.

It hadn't been a romantic setting, pushing this cumbersome old bed through the city traffic, yet it was just the kind of mad project which they both loved. It was clear from the outset that they enjoyed being together very much.

She liked his tall, rather lanky appearance, his dark tousled hair, and most of all his very sharp wit. Their courtship had followed the pattern of many student romances, with times of great uncertainty and questioning about whether they were really suited – mainly on her side.

She was an intellectual and into books: her English honours degree was deepening her love for literature and the arts. She worked to a strict timetable and if Geoff wanted to date her, she made it clear that he had to fit in with her tightly ordered work schedule.

He was an action man, more interested in people than books, and someone who always left his essays and reading to the last available moment, often working through the night to meet a deadline. He'd have spent every waking hour with her if she'd let him. He pursued her relentlessly, confident from the beginning that one day she would be his wife.

But there was another aspect to their relationship which was more difficult to define. She was attracted to him because of his faith. Both Sarah's parents were teachers, liberal intellectuals who brought her up with a 'healthy' disregard for religion in all its forms.

Her knowledge of Christianity had been strictly limited to the GCSE religious studies syllabus, and visits to church had been sparse. But she liked Geoff's quiet certainty, and was searching for a faith of her own. Her growing commitment to

Christ and her growing love for Geoff were almost inseparable; and during the eighteen months of their courtship her faith grew and matured rapidly.

The only student who had really welcomed her into the college community was Janet Winter. Janet's infectious giggle and 'fun to be with' personality drew Sarah to her. Janet's friendship had been instrumental in enabling her to understand what was happening to her spiritually. It was a relationship which Geoff never really approved of, nor fully understood. Janet Winter represented the 'evangelical' wing of college life, and he had no desire to be associated with her or her cronies. But Sarah wouldn't hear anything negative about Janet. To her, Janet was a counsellor and confidante and that was that.

Twelve months to the day after the rag week 'bed-push', Geoff proposed to Sarah. It was a well planned proposal, and Geoff had spared no expense in setting it up. They had travelled by taxi to one of the most expensive restaurants in Bristol, and were seated at a very private table for two overlooking the city's lights when he broached the subject of a 'long-term relationship'.

'We've been going out for exactly a year now, Sarah, and in a few months you'll have finished your degree and be gone. We've really found something very precious. Don't let's ever lose it.' It was quite the most difficult speech he'd ever made, but he felt confident that she'd say 'yes'.

But that was not to be. She looked out over the city skyline, afraid that he might notice her eyes filling with tears, and whispered, 'I can't say yes, Geoff ... at least, not at the moment.' The meal ended in silence, and Geoff walked her back to her digs.

Geoff never knew what happened to Sarah the night of that fateful meal. It was clear that she was upset, and somewhat confused. Sarah never did tell him where she went after he'd walked her to her digs.

But Janet Winter knew. For that night a very tearful Sarah had ended up on her doorstep, bewildered and confused and asking for help.

'Janet, I need to talk ... can I come in?'

It was well after midnight, and Janet had been asleep in bed, but the welcome was unequivocal. The two women talked until dawn, and Sarah poured out all her uncertainties about her love for Geoff. Janet sat and listened; instinctively she knew what the younger woman was asking.

'Sarah,' Janet whispered, as she gripped her hand, 'you're putting up a smoke-screen. I know what you're really asking me ... you're asking if you're a good enough Christian to marry a minister.'

There was a long silence as Sarah assimilated Janet's words.

'It's more than that, Janet. I'm not sure if I'm a Christian at all.'

'Well, if you're not sure ... make sure!' giggled Janet.

As dawn broke the two women made their way to the college chapel and in the hushed stillness of early morning Sarah knelt and gave her life to Christ. Shortly before eight o'clock that same morning she knocked on Geoff's bedsit door and whispered her 'yes'.

Geoff threw his third dart, and slowly removed all three from the dart board. He was blissfully ignorant that Janet Winter knew far more about his relationship with Sarah than anyone else; and that there was very little about his courtship and proposal which Sarah had withheld on that important night almost three years before.

Janet, who was single and romantically unattached, could only guess what kind of pressures both Geoff and Sarah were going through during those long months of separation. She knew one thing for certain. They couldn't possibly continue their commuter marriage between Gospel End and London.

'I'd do you a swop with Shetland if it would help!' she smiled, as she held out her right hand for the darts.

Geoff placed the darts firmly in her palm. 'Thanks for the thought, but I don't think it would do much good.' He smiled at the thought of Sarah and himself living on Shetland. Perhaps there were even worse options than Gospel End.

Janet Winter squinted and closed one eye in order to take aim. She rocked forward and backwards, and waved the dart to and fro in a kind of dance-like movement as she prepared to throw. Geoff bit his lip to stop himself from laughing. At last the dart was launched, landing cleanly on the students' notice board about a metre away from the dart board.

'Oh, well,' she giggled, 'I never was a very good aim. That's probably why I leave guidance to the Lord.'

Geoff cringed in disbelief. Janet Winter's theology was naive in the extreme. She couldn't even play darts without dragging God into the game. She handed back the other two darts, and Geoff breathed a sigh of relief. Had she continued to throw, he would have suggested the immediate evacuation of the common room.

It was nearly nine o'clock that evening before Sarah arrived from London. The tiny bachelor flat which Geoff occupied was filled with the strong smell of beef curry, and when she entered she saw him standing by an old cooker in a corner of the room.

'Hello, darling,' she called, throwing her bag to the floor and running to embrace him.

But Geoff was in no mood to embrace, and as quickly as he could do so he prised himself free. 'Good trip?'

'Absolutely dreadful ... but tell me. Have you heard? What's the news?'

Geoff returned to the cooker and stirred briskly. 'You're not going to like this, Sarah.'

'What do you mean? It is London ... isn't it?'

Still stirring, he muttered, 'No, it's Gospel End.'

'Gospel End? Which London borough's that in? I've never heard of it.'

'It's in the Metropolitan Borough of Great Orton in the middle of Yorkshire.'

'You've got to be joking ... but that's in the middle of nowhere!' Her voice was a mixture of sar-
casm and disbelief.

'I only wish that I was.' He spooned the rich
meaty curry over the two plates piled high with rice
and placed them both on the table in the centre of
the room. 'But if you like, I've found someone
who's willing to do a deal so that we can go to Shetland.'

'I suddenly don't feel very hungry,' she whispered, looking at the steaming dish in front of
her.

'Nor do I,' he said, pushing the untouched
plate away from him. 'Gospel End isn't exactly
what we asked for, or expected. I don't know
what to do.'

'But there must be something good about it?' She
was struggling to be positive.

'According to the principal there's an enthusiastic and supportive membership ...'

'Well, that's good.' There was a brief silence.

'But Sarah, what about your job? What about
your career? There's no way that you can commute
from Yorkshire. I just can't take this separation any
more.'

'And I suppose that dear mother church expects
me to toddle respectfully after you, Geoff, duti-
fully laying my career in the dust to further the
interests of Head Office stationing policy?'

'Yes, I think that's the gist of it.' Rather tenta-
tively he grinned at her.

'Geoffrey Notes, why couldn't you have done
something more straightforward with your life like

driving a London bus, or selling insurance ... and why did I have to go and marry someone who was already married to the church?' There was a sparkle of affection in her eyes, and she smiled warmly.

'Let's change the subject. I can't think about this any more,' he said, looking at her and watching as she swept her dark flowing hair back from her forehead. He knew again that he loved her.

Very early the following morning Sarah pulled on her jeans and T shirt and slipped silently out of the apartment to visit Janet. She was gone for nearly three hours, but Geoff was still asleep when she returned.

Her counselling session with Janet Winter didn't last long, for Janet recognised that if Sarah was to leave her job to go to Gospel End she had to make that decision herself, alone. Sarah left Janet's room with a deep feeling of disappointment. She wanted Janet to offer a decisive judgement, but it was not to be.

In the end Sarah spent most of the time alone in the college chapel, wrestling with the decision which was so wrapped up with her faith, her marriage, and her career. It was one of the loneliest vigils of her life.

When she returned to the apartment she noticed a carrier bag by the door. She opened the door and took the parcel inside. Placing the bag on the table, she pulled out a beautiful home-made candle on a pottery stand, and read the note attached: To Geoff and Sarah, Luv Janet W.

Slowly and tearfully Sarah lit the candle. She'd decided.

Chapter Two

The New Parson

Alan Drifford, sixty-seven-year-old stalwart of Gospel End Wesleyans, gripped his new minister by the elbow and pulled him away from the cluster of young wives who had surrounded him.

He led him out of the schoolroom and through the connecting door which led into the darkened sanctuary. Still gripping him by the elbow with his left hand, he turned and flicked the eight light switches with his right. The dim lighting buzzed on, revealing a pine-panelled church with fixed pews, a large circular gallery, and a very high pulpit. A smell of damp hymn books filled the air.

'Well, here it is, lad. Gospel End Wesleyans. It's been here for nearly two hundred years, and we stand in a proud tradition. All you've got to do is to fill it. And I'm quite sure that a man with your training won't find that too hard at all.'

The Reverend Geoffrey Notes smiled

graciously. Not wanting to contradict the senior layman at their first meeting, he felt it best to keep quiet. Even as he sighed, he noticed a stream of vapour rising from his mouth into the chill damp atmosphere of the church.

Already some of his worst fears about Gospel End Wesleyans were being realised. The words in the letter of introduction penned by his predecessor and marked 'Private and confidential' were more accurate than he'd imagined.

Alan Drifford turned the light switches off again, and led his reluctant new protégé back into the crowded schoolroom. Now that the cups of tea had all been distributed, the short ceremony of welcome could begin. Alan Drifford called the assembled members to order.

'... And so we've come to the chapel tonight to welcome our new minister, the Reverend Geoffrey Notes, and of course, his dear wife, er, Mrs Geoffrey Notes ... and may his stay among us at Gospel End be a very happy and fruitful one.'

A moment's poignant silence was followed by an almost spontaneous applause, led by Mr Drifford himself, whose role as senior church steward gave him an air of authority among the assembled chapel folk.

The sixty-five members of Gospel End Methodist Church – or Gospel End Wesleyans as they liked to be called – always gave their new ministers a good welcome. Mr Geoffrey Notes, like each of the thirty-seven previous Methodist ministers who had filled this appointment, had been greeted with a wave of euphoria, and the assurance that he was 'the right man for the job'.

After bidding the congregation farewell, Geoff and Sarah Notes closed the schoolroom door behind them and walked slowly back to the manse. They said nothing, but each knew the other's thoughts. The silence of disappointment hung in the air.

It wasn't as though he'd had a dramatic call to serve this little corner of God's vineyard. He was there because the National Stationing Committee hadn't been able to find anyone willing to go; and Geoffrey Notes, being a 'Probationary minister' fresh out of college, could be stationed wherever it pleased them to put him.

On this occasion it had pleased them to send him to 'Gospel End Wesleyans', a cause which many of them already knew well. It had appeared on their 'unfilled appointment' lists for many months, and because they hadn't been able to recruit a willing volunteer, they had used their powers to fill the gap with Geoffrey's name.

So, after endless committees and 'tests of his calling', after years of theological training, and months of eager anticipation, Geoffrey Notes was now the thirty-eighth incumbent of Gospel End Wesleyans. It wasn't quite what he'd expected when he'd set out on the long road to ordination. But as they trudged along the dark lane to the manse, Sarah Notes took her young husband's hand in hers and said, 'It'll be okay.'

Geoff Notes was not reassured.

Gospel End, a Yorkshire village with a history

going back to the Domesday book, was a rural community which had changed very little in over a century. It was a village which had gradually expanded over many generations, and was a town planner's nightmare – a row of thatched cottages here, a glebe of semi-detached council houses there, and in among it all some sizeable houses which had once been owned by landed gentry.

At the centre of this sprawling community there was a crossroads formed by the intersection of two B roads, neither of which went anywhere important. The crossroads was overshadowed by four large buildings, each of which was tall and imposing.

On one side was the grocery store, which had been owned and managed by the Field family for three generations and where you could buy anything from a hat-pin to a postal order. Opposite was the village school, which had successfully fought off every threat of closure from an increasingly militant local education authority.

The other two 'prime sites' were filled by those bastions of community life, the chapel and the public house. The Fox and Hounds had a history going back more than three hundred years. It was the kind of public house which 'froze out' strangers; it was also the main gathering point for the menfolk of the village. Stan Menston, the owner and landlord, was a very big man who huffed and puffed his way around the bar. He ruled his pub with a rod of iron. His customers, his tiny wife Molly and his two Rottweilers, 'Gin' and 'Tonic', treated him with the greatest respect.

Facing the pub was the chapel, with its imposing

frontage, complete with a cross on the gable end and a stained-glass window – the only church in the village. The Anglicans hadn't had much of a look-in since John Wesley had ridden into town in 1756 and precipitated a 'revival of religion' which had led to the eventual closure of the Anglican church and the formation of a Methodist 'Class Meeting'.

The tall edifice of the chapel faced the public house head on: architecturally the two buildings stood on either side of the street shouting menacingly at each other. The Wesleyan commitment to total abstinence had led to generations of ill-feeling between the two institutions. They represented two distinct halves of village life; the chapel was predominantly attended by the village womenfolk, while the public house entertained the men.

Geoff's first major mistake at Gospel End was made on his second day as its minister, and revealed a total lack of understanding of this underlying tension in the life of the village. He was a city boy, brought up in an easy-going inner London church, and trained in one of the denomination's most progressive colleges.

To him, dropping into the pub for a lager was the most natural way of making contact with the people of the local community. Sarah decided to join him. The house-move and ensuing chaos meant that the house didn't feel like home yet, and the thought of a quiet evening together in a country pub was attractive to both of them.

They pushed open the door of the public bar and walked confidently in. It was early evening, and about a dozen men were talking loudly in several small groups. By the time Geoff and Sarah had reached the bar, however, all conversation had ceased and they were being eyed coldly by all the regulars of the Fox and Hounds.

Geoff ordered two low-alcohol lagers. Molly, the landlord's wife, smiled politely and poured the drinks. Geoff and Sarah took their drinks and sat together in the bay window overlooking the church. As they looked out of the window at the imposing structure opposite, they gradually became aware of the whispering all around them. It was clear that they were the new subject of conversation at the Fox and Hounds.

At that moment the door behind the bar burst open, and Stan Menston strode in, followed meekly by Tonic, the larger of his two Rottweilers. He wheezed as he lifted the bar barrier and walked through, and then gasped his way from table to table collecting empty glasses, until four were grasped in each hand. At last he arrived at the bay-window table, looked down on the young couple, and muttered, 'Are you the new man at chapel, then?'

'Why, yes, I am,' said Geoff, almost apologetically. 'I'm very pleased to meet you.' He held out his right hand, and then withdrew it with embarrassment. You can't give four beer mugs the right hand of fellowship. 'And this is my wife, Sarah. We've only just moved in.'

All the regulars were now facing the couple and standing in anticipation, like an audience, waiting for Stan's next line. They half expected him to ask the new parson to leave, or at least to offer some mocking comment about the church turning to drink. He spent time taking breath, as if weighing up the new parson and deciding what to say.

'You're welcome, lad ... come here any time ... and the next drink's on me. Let me introduce you round.' And, in a matter of moments, Geoffrey Notes was shaking hands with all the regulars and the buzz of normal conversation returned. He quickly became so engrossed in conversation that he didn't notice what had happened to Sarah. She was seated alone in the window seat, and was red with embarrassment.

The welcome to the Fox and Hounds had not been extended to her, for she was a woman and a parson's wife. Even the regulars at the Fox and Hounds had their standards, and the bounds of cordial welcome could not extend that far. It was a full half-hour before she finally caught his eye and he knew at once that it was time to leave.

Geoff was flushed with success as they walked back home from the pub; he felt that the local community had already begun to take him to its heart – and that, after all, Gospel End wasn't such a bad place in which to begin his ministry. Sarah was alone in her thoughts. For even now, only days after her arrival at Gospel End, she felt isolated. It seemed there was no place for her in either half of village life, the chapel or the pub. To make matters worse, Geoff was already so engrossed in his new ministry at Gospel End that she felt increasingly frozen out of her relationship with him as well.

The early days of Geoff Notes' ministry at Gospel End were filled with a breathtaking attempt to visit every member of the congregation in their own home, a task which for once he planned precisely, and which he tackled with his usual charming manner. Within a matter of days he had transferred the church membership list from the battered card index he'd inherited onto the green screen of his new Amstrad 8256 word-processor. He had plotted the spread of his congregation throughout the village community by sticking small green pins into a large brown map of the area, which was now irrevocably impaled to the wall of his cluttered study.

Many of the church members were elderly, and he had to admit that sometimes conversation with them was plain hard work. He discovered that the simple question 'How are you?' could turn on a stream of stories about operations, doctors and remedies which was hard to turn off again. The detail with which Mrs Jones of Brow Edge could describe her mastectomy startled him. She was stirring her spoon in her china cup, and the more the story unfolded, the faster she seemed to stir. As she described the operation itself the waves of tea lapped over her cup and into the saucer, dissolving her rich tea biscuit into a soggy brown mass.

'Another coconut slice, Mr Notes?' she asked, as she put down the teacup and held out a plate of cakes for his approval. 'I only made them this morning ... I thought you might be popping round today.'

Geoff Notes bit into his coconut slice, and wondered how she could have predicted his visit so accurately. Perhaps, he mused, she was a secret computer hacker and had cracked the password to his secret visiting schedule? He dismissed the thought. It seemed rather more possible, however, that she had other, older ways, of knowing where he was and what he was doing.

'And your wife, Mr Notes?' she asked sympathetically. 'How is she settling in?'

Unaware of the importance of the question Geoff assured Mrs Jones that Sarah liked the village, was settling in well, and was looking for a job. The old lady leaned forward, determined to remember the exact wording of the answer, an answer which might be taken down and later used in evidence.

It was only as Geoff was half-way through his second coconut slice that he gazed up at the picture frame above the fireplace, and saw a very old certificate with ornate religious script. In large letters at the top of the certificate were the words 'Band of Hope', and underneath the inscription 'Certificate of Merit: Gospel End Wesleyans'. He had never seen anything quite like it before. Total abstinence was clearly something which had figured prominently in the history of the Gospel End Church.

As Geoff began to make his farewell speech to the old lady in the chair, a speech he had already given many times during his short stay in the village, he became aware that his words were not being received in quite the way he'd hoped. He ploughed on.

'... as I say, Mrs Jones, all you have to do is to telephone me if you need anything, and I'll be happy to call.'

'Perhaps you'd see yourself out,' Mrs Jones

replied. 'Your predecessor always saw himself out. *He* visited every week, not just by request.'

Geoff bit his lip. He did not want to end this first pastoral visit with Mrs Jones on a note of controversy. He had no intention of visiting this particular member every week, no matter how delicious her coconut slices were, but perhaps this was not the moment to tell her so. He drove back home, wondering how Sarah was getting on with job hunting; they needed her salary to make ends meet.

As he drove back through the centre of the village he noticed that Alan Drifford, the senior church steward, was engrossed in conversation with Steven Jenkins, the church property secretary. Both men were clad in dirty overalls. They were both looking upwards at the roof, and Steve Jenkins was pointing up at the eaves and explaining something very complicated.

On an impulse, Geoff indicated left, and pulled up outside the church. He got out of the car and called, 'Good afternoon, gentlemen, have we got problems?'

Alan was obviously embarrassed. The information he had just received was too devastating to share with anyone yet. He needed time to ponder it, think it through, and come to some conclusion with his old friend Steve. He certainly wasn't ready to face the new minister.

'Oh, no, Mr Notes, everything is fine. We're just looking over the premises as part of our quinquennial inspection. We have to keep Head Office happy, you know!' The other official grunted in agreement.

It was at that precise moment that Stan Menston emerged from the Fox and Hounds, followed by Gin and Tonic. He was holding a walking cane with an ornate golden handle, about to set out on his daily constitutional. He paused and looked across the road. 'Hello there, Geoff, how's tricks?'

Alan Drifford and Steven Jenkins were flabbergasted. What they had just witnessed horrified them. That the publican should address their minister at all was unheard of ... but to call him by his Christian name, and to ask 'How's tricks'! They would never dream of addressing a minister of the cloth in such a way.

'Fine, Stan,' retorted Geoff. 'How's business? I'll be taking you up on that offer of a lager tonight.'

The senior steward and the property secretary looked at each other in amazement. They were speechless with indignation. How could their minister, the official representative of Gospel End Wesleyans, enquire about the state of business at the Fox and Hounds? They felt sure that out of all the thirty-seven previous incumbents of this church there had never been one who was on first-name terms with the publican at the Fox and Hounds. The chapel folk and the regulars at the Fox and Hounds lived in separate worlds, side by side.

Satisfied that his two loyal church members were telling the truth about the property, Geoffrey Notes bade them farewell and got back into his car. He seemed blithely unaware that as he drove away he left them standing there, frozen with astonishment.

As good as his word, Geoffrey Notes made his second visit to the Fox and Hounds later that night. Sarah excused herself, saying she wanted to read, so Geoff went alone. It was darts night at the Fox and Hounds and the regulars were gathered around the dart board, glasses in hands, commenting shrewdly on each throw.

Without pausing to reflect on the implications Geoff agreed to play a game. The dart board in his college common room had been a gathering point for Geoff's particular group of friends; and some days he'd done more darts than theology. By the third throw it was clear that all those years in theological college hadn't been wasted; Geoff's dart-playing expertise drew gasps of approval from the regulars standing around him.

Stan Menston placed a firm hand on Geoff's shoulder, handed him a second free glass of low-alcohol lager, and wheezed, 'You're just the chap we need to join our team.'

There was no conversation on the matter and certainly no opportunity to decline. Stan's statement was as binding as a Royal Decree and the regulars all concurred approvingly. To withdraw now would jeopardise Geoff's relationship with them all for ever.

The glasses were raised. Stan Menston coughed and spluttered, and then proposed a toast. 'To Geoff, our parson and darts team champ.'

Out in the darkness, safe behind the garden wall of the chapel, Alan Drifford, the senior church steward of Gospel End Wesleyans, stood and watched. He had a perfect view through the large bay window of the Fox and Hounds. As he watched, a sense of anger rose within him such as he'd never known before.

Of all the parsons he'd ever served under, he'd never known any of them let the side down in quite this way. Alan Drifford now had two problems to occupy his mind. The premises, and the parson. He needed advice from someone older and wiser than himself. He got into his car and drove away to see his mentor, Mrs Jones up at Brow Edge.

Geoff didn't stay much longer at the Fox and Hounds. As soon as the darts game was over he walked back home, and as he sauntered up the garden path he saw the figure of his wife Sarah, silhouetted at the bedroom window. She stood motionless, staring outwards towards the lights of the Fox and Hounds.

He turned the key and went inside. Creeping quietly into the bedroom he stood behind her and whispered, 'Darling, what's wrong?'

'Oh, nothing.' She sighed, and turned to face him. He took her gently in his arms, and as he held her, he became aware of her delicate vulnerability. She was clinging on to him, grasping for security. She was hiding the truth from him, aware that the intensity of her unhappiness might be too much for him to bear just then.

That evening, while he'd been playing darts at the Fox and Hounds, she had been writing a long and heartfelt letter to Janet Winter in Shetland. She really needed help.

She described the unfriendly chapel people,

worlds apart from her trendy colleagues in London publishing, and the night at the Fox and Hounds, when she'd felt frozen out of the conversation. She confessed to Janet that she'd never felt lonelier in her life, and wondered why God had allowed her to end up at a place like Gospel End. Geoff never knew about the letter, or its contents; and he would never fully understand Sarah's need of a pastor.

'Good news,' he whispered. 'I'm the new member of the Fox and Hounds' darts team. I'm really getting to the heart of this community, I can feel it.'

Even as he spoke, it seemed she clung more tightly. As if there weren't enough pressures in the church. Did he really have to join a darts team too? She knew one thing for sure: she'd never darken the doors of the Fox and Hounds again – it was as unwelcoming a place as Gospel End Wesleyans.

As he held her in his arms, he gazed out of the window at the lights in the street outside. Already he was beginning to love this little community called Gospel End, and already he was beginning to feel a part of it.

Across on the other side of the village, Mr Alan Drifford was consuming his third coconut slice. Mrs Jones had assumed her forward sitting posture, her 'I'll not miss a single word' position. Alan was now in full flow, giving a detailed account of the scenes he'd witnessed through the window of the Fox and Hounds earlier that evening. Every new revelation seemed to bring a greater look of horror across the face of Mrs Jones. She nodded and tutted and sighed as every detail unfolded. This was indeed a serious matter, and she was grateful that Alan Drifford had felt it right to confide in her.

Meanwhile, among the clinking beer mugs and friendly chatter at the Fox and Hounds, Stan Menston was silently congratulating himself that, after all these years, the Fox and Hounds had found respectability at last. Many of his regulars were married to chapel women; and many of them knew the daily grind of having to excuse themselves for having frequented 'that place' again. But Stan knew that if the Methodist parson became a regular, the women of the chapel could be silenced for ever.

Slowly, almost imperceptibly, the news about Geoff's secondment to the Fox and Hounds' darts team spread from house to house around the village. One of the first to hear the news was Mrs Field, whose position behind the post-office counter gave her an unrivalled opportunity to receive and to pass on what was happening within the tiny community. As she was neither a member of the chapel nor a regular at the Fox and Hounds she had to tread carefully. Automatically, she conveyed the latest news in measured terms to the different customers at the other side of her security window.

To the chapel people she spoke in deep tones of regret and distaste, like the passing of some news about a fatal motor accident, or some terminal illness. But to the people who frequented the Fox and Hounds she spoke with sparkling eyes, and a smirk of humour. She knew that the appointment of the Rev Geoffrey Notes to the Fox and Hounds' darts team had very real implications for everyone at Gospel End.

Chapter Three

Property Matters

All but one of the Gospel End Wesleyan Property Committee arrived punctually for their seven thirty meeting. Alan Drifford unlocked the door to the schoolroom at seven twenty-nine and the six ageing members of the committee followed him into the dimly lit room. They took off their coats and sat on a neat row of tubular metal chairs in front of a table.

The table was reserved for the Reverend Geoffrey Notes. As chairman of all the committees at Gospel End he had the privilege of sitting behind the table and following the Agenda which was always courteously provided by Alan Drifford at the start of each meeting. Generations of ministers had accepted this situation without question. None of them, however, had ever realised that this state of affairs put them at a severe disadvantage in the invisible power struggle between the minister and the lay folk at Gospel End.

The committee remained seated, talking politely to one another in hushed whispers, like children awaiting the arrival of a fierce class teacher. At precisely seven thirty-five the schoolroom door burst open and a breathless Geoffrey Notes, making profuse apologies about 'an urgent phone call', took off his top coat and hung it on the row of coat pegs by the door. A natural 'group dynamics' man, he lifted the small chairman's table to one side, and urged everyone to 'form a tight circle of chairs'. Obedient as ever, the little band of committee buffs pulled their chairs into a circle. Mr Drifford did not have to move, because the circle formed automatically on either side of him.

Alan Drifford, acting on the advice of his mentor Mrs Jones, had called the meeting. He'd decided that he couldn't tackle the problems of property and parson at once.

'After all,' Mrs Jones had cautioned, 'the Reverend Notes has only been here a fortnight. We can hardly have a show-down already. You'd better deal with the property first.'

So he ignored the unusual drinking habits of the new parson, at least for the present, and concentrated on the problems of the property. His recent inspection of the premises with the property secretary Steven Jenkins had caused him deep concern, and he knew that something had to be done quickly. The current crisis had arisen when Steven Jenkins had discovered, during his five-yearly inspection of the eaves and the chapel loft, that extensive wet rot had developed. Shining his torch around the darkest corners of the roof joists, he had discovered that the rot was so extensive that the roof was quite beyond repair.

Alan Drifford, devastated by the quinquennial report, had then joined Steven Jenkins for a more detailed inspection on the fateful afternoon when the new parson had spotted them gazing up at the eaves. Their prolonged inspection had revealed that damp had seeped into many parts of the church structure, and that the ceiling above the main sanctuary was in imminent danger of collapse.

For many years Alan Drifford's general attitude to church property had been 'make do and mend'; and throughout his long reign at Gospel End Wesleyans he had never spent two pounds when one would do. It seemed, at last, that the day of reckoning for this lack of foresight would soon be upon him. If only, he thought miserably, he had registered that the smell of stale hymn books was indicative of something important. If only he had taken the complaints of 'dampness' seriously from ageing church members. If only he had called in an expert to deal with the small patch of wet rot identified at the quinquennial inspection five years previously.

Alan Drifford's years of church administration had prepared him well for this extraordinary meeting of the Property Committee. The six members of the committee had been entertained to tea at his home prior to the meeting, and Mrs Drifford had furnished them with a delicious ham salad. The outcome of the Property Committee meeting was fully decided by the time Mrs Drifford had carried the empty plates back to the kitchen. Geoffrey

Notes, of course, was a young innocent abroad, and oblivious of such practices in local church affairs.

Once the circle had formed, and the scraping of chairs had ceased, Geoff Notes prayed a sincere prayer for guidance. He then looked down at the scrap of paper handed to him by Alan Drifford and which read 'Property Committee Agenda'.

'Well,' said Geoff, 'it looks as though our meeting together shouldn't last long – with only one matter for discussion on the agenda.' The naivety of the young minister was obvious to everyone in the group. 'What do you all really feel about asking for a Government Preservation Order on our property?' he continued brightly. 'My own view is that a Preservation Order will do nothing but restrict us if we ever want to change the image of our property.'

He had underestimated the opposition. Alan Drifford kicked off with a well reasoned speech about the historic importance of Gospel End Wesleyans, and of their need to preserve the chapel for future generations. Others in the group added various statements of support. It was at this precise moment that Geoffrey Notes realised that, as the impartial chairman of the meeting, he could hardly steer the business his way. While everything within him questioned the wisdom of seeking a Preservation Order, he felt powerless to oppose it. With failing courage he felt that it was safer to rubber-stamp the proposal than dare to disagree with the members. He was surprised to discover that Alan Drifford, who had the application forms with him already, was urging the meeting to 'sign them here and now'. Isolated and alone, Geoff felt powerless to prevent the application from being made.

The forms were signed, and after a brief word of benediction the seven members of the Property Committee trudged out of the schoolroom. Geoff donned his coat, closed the schoolroom door, and climbed into his car. It was barely seven forty-five. He felt uneasy. It had all been a bit too straightforward.

Alan Drifford and Steven Jenkins went immediately to Brow Edge, where Mrs Jones was already waiting with the kettle boiling. She wanted a full report of all that had happened. Over hot tea and her last remaining coconut slices they described the meeting in every detail.

'Well done,' she concluded. 'Perhaps Mr Notes won't be such a problem, after all.'

It seemed that Geoffrey Notes' popularity at the Fox and Hounds grew with every visit he made. His first darts match was to be played on home ground against one of the toughest pubs in the league, the Coach and Horses. The men of the Coach and Horses had won the trophy for three consecutive years; an honour which had only ever been equalled once, when the men of the Fox and Hounds had won the trophy from 1956 to 1959. It was a matter of the greatest importance that the Coach and Horses should not win a fourth time; and that, if at all possible, the honour of the Fox and Hounds should be vindicated with a clear win.

Darts players, like sportsmen of every kind, occasionally have a winning streak. The competition against the Coach and Horses was just such a night for Geoff Notes. It seemed that he could do nothing wrong. Three bull's-eyes in rapid succession made some of the players from the Coach and Horses wonder if this parson had some assistance from the Almighty in his accurate aim and steady throw.

The regulars at the Fox and Hounds beamed with pride. Geoff Notes was a hero. Never, in all their years of darts competitions, had they acquired a player of such calibre. It seemed, at long last, that the winning streak of the Coach and Horses might be ended – and that the Fox and Hounds might recapture the cup, and return it to its rightful place on a ledge behind their bar, a ledge which had remained empty for more than six years.

Geoff made the last throw and, as the regulars watched with bated breath, he soundly won the competition with his deadly accuracy. The cheering was ecstatic.

Stan Menston and all the regulars joined in a toast to further victories in the ensuing rounds of the competition. Stan then toasted 'the good losers' at the Coach and Horses and triggered a murmur of remorse from the visiting team.

Next, Stan and all the regulars at the Fox and Hounds raised their glasses in the direction of their new champ, Geoffrey Notes; and Stan led off with a wheezing rendition of 'for he's a jolly good fellow'. Riding on the euphoria of the moment Geoff thanked everyone for 'a darn good match', and reminded them that it was Harvest Festival on Sunday.

'One good turn deserves another,' he smiled. 'Why not come and support my team across the road?'

Geoff left the pub with a lightness of step, and a renewed sense of purpose. If the regulars from the Fox and Hounds arrived at the Gospel End Wesleyan Harvest Festival he would have brought off the greatest coup in many years. He was getting to the heart of this community all right. He could really feel it.

Sarah, too, was feeling slightly happier, having made her first friend at Gospel End. Sarah Notes and Jenny Drifford, Alan's daughter, first met in Field's grocery store when Jenny apologised for her absence from the welcome meeting. At last, Sarah had met someone to whom she could relate, and readily accepted Jenny's invitation to call round for coffee on Wednesday evening. Immediately the two women got on well.

Jenny, an attractive blonde twenty-seven-year-old, had graduated in Environmental Studies at Durham University. She was now an area sales representative for a rapidly expanding health-food company, and travelled to food shops throughout the north in her Vauxhall Cavalier. Marriage had so far eluded her, and she lived alone in a newly refurbished cottage near the centre of the village. She was probably too confident for any of the men from Gospel End to dare approach her. Although a committed Christian, she found the intrigues of Gospel End Wesleyans hard to accept, and was slowly moving toward the fringes of church life.

As Sarah slowly sipped Cambodian coffee that dark Wednesday evening, she invited her new friend, Jenny, to help design the Gospel End harvest display. Plans for the Gospel End Harvest Festival followed a traditional pattern. It was customary for the minister's wife to arrange the display and, feeling it was something she could do with artistic flair, Sarah Notes had readily agreed to take on this particular role. She had been looking for someone like Jenny to bounce her ideas off. Jenny was enthusiastic, and in a matter of minutes the ideas were flowing. They had similar views on things, and it wasn't long before they agreed that the festival display should take on a revolutionary new shape.

Their idea was certainly different. They planned to stack the pulpit side of the communion area with harvest produce but to leave the lectern side of the chapel bare, save for a glass of brown water, and a small bag of rice. They felt that the contrast would speak volumes.

The members of Gospel End were somewhat reassured by Sarah's eagerness to be involved in the harvest, and were pleased to hear that she had invited Jenny Drifford to assist her. Alan Drifford was particularly thrilled that his daughter had been afforded the high honour of assisting the minister's wife with the harvest display.

Between ten am and twelve noon on Saturday morning the chapel was a-buzz with activity. It was one of those very dark, wet, October days, and the streets were full of puddles. Gospel End had always had a problem with drainage. Piles of produce from farms, allotments, gardens, and supermarket shelves were carried in by the dripping souls of Gospel End. Umbrellas were shaken, rain-macs were taken off, and everyone complained about the weather.

The Field sisters, elderly spinsters whose brother owned the general store, brought in tomatoes, carrots, and a large marrow. Their marrow traditionally formed the focus of the display. They were keen gardeners, and the Harvest Festival gave them a rare opportunity to display their skills.

Jenny Drifford was engrossed in arranging a display of vegetarian and health-food products on a shelf beneath the pulpit. She was firmly committed to green issues, and felt that the focus of the 'bounty' side of the display should be a large bowl of free-range eggs.

Local farmer Brian Selhurst entered with a large sheaf of corn under each arm, followed by his strapping twenty-eight-year-old son John who was carrying a sack of potatoes on his shoulder. Mr Selhurst and his son stood looking puzzled. It was quite the oddest harvest display they'd ever seen.

'Shall I put a sheaf either side of the chapel like normal?' Brian asked innocently, the rain dripping down his cheeks. 'It's looking a bit bare around the lectern.'

'No, thank you,' said Jenny. 'We're working to a design, you see, and we'll need both sheaves on the pulpit side this year.'

Mr Selhurst Senior, still holding the sheaves of corn, looked aghast at the diverse range of vegetarian and health-food produce arranged beneath the pulpit. Then he spotted a large sign beside a bowl of eggs which made his blood boil. It read simply, 'Organic farming is here to stay.' Without a moment's hesitation, he strode out of the chapel with the sheaves of corn still under his arms. As he went, he muttered, 'I'll be seeing you, then.' His views on organic farming didn't bear repeating.

Brian's son John, never known for his sensitivity, dumped the sack of potatoes beside the glass of brown water and the packet of rice. He strode out whistling 'We plough the fields and scatter'. Speechless, Sarah Notes just stood and watched. 'Don't worry about them,' smiled Jenny, 'they're always like that.'

A very wet Geoff Notes arrived as the last touches were being added to the 'bounty' side of the display. He was most impressed.

'That's brilliant, girls ... well done.' Sarah and Jenny stood beside him and admired their hand-iwork. It really did look good.

Alan Drifford arrived to lock the chapel, and after seeing Geoff, Sarah and Jenny safely off the premises, he went back inside to look at the display. He couldn't believe his eyes. If it wasn't for Jenny's involvement in the project, he would have rear-ranged the display there and then. He sighed with despair and turned to face the driving rain. What were they playing at? How could they spoil the annual harvest display?

The rain continued incessantly. It was the heaviest downpour for many months and the village street was deserted. The sheets of rain blew across the village, funnelled, it seemed, towards the roof of Gospel End Wesleyans. Silently, the weakened joists swelled with the weight of water. The crisis in the property was rapidly coming to a head.

It was still drizzling at eight o'clock on Sunday morning, when Alan Drifford opened up the chapel doors and checked the boiler. He looked again at the display and wondered how his daughter could have been so insensitive to the traditions of the chapel folk.

At ten fifteen Steven Jenkins, who was on hymn-book duty that morning, shook his umbrella and stood by the front door of the chapel ready to greet the flock. Geoff Notes was getting into his cassock in the rear vestry, a ritual which Alan Drifford watched with some disdain. He approved of preaching gowns, but felt that cassocks were inappropriate attire at Gospel End.

Slowly the dripping congregation began to gather. Harvest Festival always brought a good turn-out of the faithful, and there was a healthy spread of ages from children to octogenarians. Mrs Jones of Brow Edge hobbled in, supported by the two Field sisters, on one of her rare appearances at church. She hated to miss the harvest display.

It would be wrong to say that the harvest display upset everyone. Many of the congregation saw it as an interesting and imaginative departure from tradition, but for some of the inner core of the fellowship it was a big disappointment. For decades the display had followed a similar pattern and this concoction didn't seem like harvest. Several people remarked on the absence of the Selhurst family and the lack of harvest sheaves which usually featured in the display. The Field sisters were sad that their prize marrow was obscured by the display of wholefood, and said as much to Mrs Jones, who was seated between them, looking annoyed.

At ten fifty-nine precisely, as the volume of the organ voluntary was steadily rising in anticipation of the start of the service, Steve Jenkins peered out into the rain in disbelief. For striding across the road from the Fox and Hounds was Stan Menston, followed by his wife Molly. The publican from the Fox and Hounds had not darkened the doors of the Wesleyans for a very long time.

Steve handed them hymn books and greeted them with the words, "Mornin', 'ave an 'imbook.' It was obvious that both Stan and Molly felt embarrassed. Stan had swallowed two strong whiskies before he felt up to the ordeal. He had not been inside the church for more than twenty years – and even then it had been to pay his last respects at the funeral of a regular. Geoff's victory at the darts match had made a significant impact on Stan, however, and he felt that by attending church he might encourage the lad.

The Menstons were barely seated before the congregation was on its feet and singing 'Come, ye thankful people, come'. Stan, wheezing as usual, sang out the words with considerable gusto. He'd always liked singing.

Mrs Jones of Brow Edge was puzzled to know who owned the breathless baritone and, on looking round, she gasped in disbelief. She nudged the

Miss Fields on either side of her. 'Look who's come to church, then.' They too turned, and stared. The presence of Stan Menston in the chapel was almost too shocking and painful for Mrs Jones to bear, and if she had been able she would have walked out in disgust.

The unorthodox display and the presence of the two new members of the congregation completely preoccupied Alan Drifford's thoughts. He hadn't even noticed that in the 'bounty' half of the display a small pool of water was gathering beside the bowl of tomatoes. It was formed by the incessant dripping of water from a crack in the ceiling.

After reading a prayer, Geoffrey Notes formally announced the second hymn, 'We plough the fields and scatter', which the congregation began to sing with great enthusiasm.

> He sends the snow in winter,
> The warmth to swell the grain,
> The breezes and the sunshine,
> And soft refreshing rain:

As if on cue, and with great dramatic irony, a large section of ceiling plaster collapsed as they sang the word 'rain'. A sodden mixture of dust, water and splinters descended like a flurry of snow and covered much of the harvest produce. Most of the congregation fell silent; but the organist, blithely unaware of what had happened, played on. Stan Menston continued, unabashed.

All good gifts around us
Are sent from heaven above;
Then thank the Lord, O thank the Lord,
For all his love.

Chapter Four

The Inheritance

As Sarah and Geoff washed up together after lunch on the day of the fateful harvest service, their conversation turned to Sarah's role at Gospel End. It was one of those conversations which they both knew was significant, though completely unplanned.

'I'm pleased you're getting on well with Jenny,' said Geoff, his hands immersed in a steaming bowl of soapy water. 'You're going to need some real friends.'

'Yes,' said Sarah, piling the plates into an old green kitchen unit, 'without Jenny, I'm not sure how long I could take all this.'

Geoff slowly wiped the cutlery with a dishcloth and turned to face her. 'What do you mean?'

'This village, this "Gospel End Wesleyans".' Her bitterness was unmistakable.

'But they've made us very welcome ... '

Sarah interrupted. 'They've made *you* very welcome. You've got a role in the chapel – and even in the village. But me? It's as though I don't exist. If Gospel End Wesleyans treat all newcomers like they've treated me, it's little wonder they're a dying cause.'

'But what about Jenny?' Geoff said, almost apologetically.

'Jenny's different,' Sarah admitted, 'she's for real. The others treat me like some kind of adjunct to you ... they even welcomed me as Mrs Geoff Notes. I am a *person*, I do have a *name*.' She was near to tears. This little storm had evidently been brewing for some time.

She paused to take breath. Geoff turned back to the pile of dishes and began to splash the soapy suds again. They both needed to break the tension. Sarah took up the tea towel again and sighed.

'There's something fundamentally wrong with that church, Geoff, and you can't even see it. There's a power structure so strong ... so protective of its own interests ... that I doubt if you'll ever break it.'

'But it's early days yet,' he said optimistically. 'With time I'm sure that I can help them to become less introverted and more welcoming. These people all seem to hurt so much, I think they need to be loved ... and taught.'

'Well, Geoff, you may be willing to give the next five years of your life to the needs of Gospel End Wesleyans, but I'm really not sure if I can. There are more pressing needs, bigger issues. The world's falling apart, and all that lot can worry about is the church roof.'

Silence. Geoff knew this wasn't the moment for a counter-attack.

'It's just like that letter said,' she continued, enjoying her winning streak, 'the one your predecessor left on the mantelpiece ... you might as well forget it ... it's all a waste of time. He told you that they destroyed him and warned you that they'd do the same to you. Why don't you ever listen, Geoff?'

Check-mate. The letter was irrefutable evidence. He pulled the last saucepan out of the water, and held it above the bowl until the dripping ceased.

'How about a cup of tea?' For Geoff, the conversation was over and he couldn't take any more ... not just then.

On Monday morning at about nine am on the day after the harvest catastrophe, Mr and Mrs Drifford drove over to Brow Edge. They both knew how important it was to seek Mrs Jones' advice on things. They wanted her to tell them what to say at the emergency Property Committee meeting to be held later that morning. Alan Drifford always liked to keep Mrs Jones up to date with developments. If she heard any news about the Wesleyans second-hand, through someone in the village, she was deeply wounded. For many years she had invisibly steered the business of all the church committees at Gospel End, using Alan Drifford and Steven Jenkins as her emissaries.

Alan knocked on the back door. It was always left open, but he would never dream of entering without hearing the familiar call 'Come in, dear'.

Mrs Drifford turned to admire the roses on the large bush beside the cottage step. There was no response, even after a second knock, so Alan pushed open the door and called nervously, 'Mrs Jones? It's only me!'

They waited several more minutes before daring to enter the house. They moved from room to room, as if on tiptoe, and called, 'Hello, Mrs Jones' as if to excuse their intrusion. At last they found her in her bedroom. Her cold, still body was lying, as if asleep, on the bed. They knew immediately that she was dead, but, as if to make sure, Alan touched the frozen hand outstretched on the counterpane. Mrs Jones had died in her sleep. As if in a dream he telephoned the doctor, but assured him that there was no need to hurry.

Mr and Mrs Drifford and Steven Jenkins arrived at the chapel promptly at eleven am that same Monday morning. Alan Drifford's mind was numbed by the shock of the morning's events, but he'd decided to keep the news to himself until the moment seemed right. Mrs Drifford disappeared into the chapel kitchen. Property was men's business.

The display of harvest bounty was still in place in the sanctuary, and it was still covered by dust and plaster. No one had been allowed to enter until this inspection had given the 'all clear'. Geoff Notes and local builder Jack Allinson of 'Allinson and Nephew' were already in the main sanctuary, standing beneath the hole in the ceiling and staring upwards. Drifford and Jenkins entered with the bearing of naughty schoolboys who'd been found out for committing some minor misdemeanour. Geoff was cast in the role of schoolmaster, angry that those deputed to care for the property had allowed it to deteriorate so badly. Without the presence of Jack Allinson the builder, who was not a 'chapel man', his observations would have been undiplomatically blunt.

Geoff opened the proceedings. 'It's a good job that no one was killed and it's quite clear that there are major problems with this building. We need to know, and know now, just how unsafe this structure really is.'

Geoff's manner was firm and uncompromising, an unusual stance for a minister at Gospel End. There was even a hint of anger in his voice. Drifford and Jenkins were silenced ... they had never had to deal with an angry minister before.

The foursome spent much of the morning clambering deep into the bowels of the Gospel End Chapel. They crawled into all the nooks and crannies which large buildings have, but which are rarely seen. Every few moments they paused, while Jack Allinson dictated his verdict into a tiny hand-held dictaphone.

'Roof, extensive wet rot. Main joists weak. Ceiling, dangerous. Evidence of rain seeping through roof. Urgent rewiring required. Danger of rain affecting worn cables.'

They moved on to the cellar, the boiler-house, and even the dark dusty store-hole beneath the schoolroom stage. And after each inspection, after each torch-lit revelation, each round of tuts and sighs, there was the verdict, a clipped, precise, technical statement which made Alan Drifford's heart sink lower still. It was nearly one o'clock by the time they had finished, and they returned to the schoolroom looking like coal miners after a hard shift.

Mrs Drifford, who'd been doing some cleaning in the kitchen, emerged with a tray of tea and biscuits. She always knew when Alan really needed support, and this was one of those days. The four sat back on their chairs and drank their tea in silence. The three chapel men looked into their teacups and felt awkward.

At last Jack Allinson broke the silence, because he had another pressing engagement. He spoke in short clipped phrases, as if he was still speaking into his dictaphone.

'I am sorry to say this. These premises are dangerous. You're lucky that no one was injured on Sunday and you should take that as a warning. The whole roof of the main sanctuary is liable to collapse; and the extensive wet rot beneath this schoolroom floor means that this building isn't safe, either. Poor drainage has always been a problem in this town, and that's at the root of it all. To put this lot right you're talking hundreds of thousands of pounds ... and to be honest, gentlemen, you'd be throwing good money after bad. These premises have had their day. They're a liability.'

Geoff Notes, always able to act the diplomat when he had to, cleared his throat as if he were about to address a huge gathering.

'Thank-you for your honesty, Mr Allinson. You

could easily have persuaded us to patch up the ceiling, but I appreciate your professional assessment of the situation.' Drifford and Jenkins stared in silence.

Jack Allinson offered further help, should it be required, and beat a hasty departure. The remaining three looked back into their teacups. Eye contact wasn't easy.

'Have you posted that application for a Preservation Order?' Geoff asked, looking up, at last, from his tea.

'Yes,' said Alan, still looking down.

'Then first we must recall the Property Committee, and get them to revoke their decision. The last thing we need on this place is a Preservation Order; it'll ruin the lot of us. We can only hope that the Council doesn't take action on this. It's obvious to me that the Property Committee was not presented with all the facts. It's quite disgraceful. We must withdraw that order. Agreed?'

'Agreed,' the other two replied in unison. Neither had the stomach for a fight, not just then. Geoff was pleasantly surprised; this was proving easier than he'd imagined.

'And as a result of Allinson's report, do we agree that we declare these premises unsafe, and seek to worship elsewhere, for the time being?'

Alan Drifford looked up, as if to say something, but he couldn't find a word to say. He was still reeling from all the events of the day.

'Agreed,' said Jenkins.

'I suppose ... if there's no alternative,' Drifford submitted, 'but on one condition.'

'And what is that?' asked Geoff, treating the statement as rather impertinent.

'That we hold the funeral here. It won't hurt if we come in once more, will it, just for a few minutes?' There was a pathetic pleading attitude in Alan Drifford's bearing.

'And whose funeral is that?' asked Geoff blankly.

Alan straightened his back: the bearer of more bad news, he had a duty to perform. 'Why, Mrs Jones, of course,' he said. 'She died last night. I thought you knew.'

Geoff's mouth fell open. He couldn't think of anything to say. 'I'm sorry,' he muttered at last: the death of the chapel, and the death of its oldest member, seemed strangely interlinked.

Mrs Drifford collected the cups. The meeting was over. They'd all had as much as they could take for one morning. They emerged into the bright sunlight of the October day and went their separate ways.

Alan Drifford pushed his garden gate open, and then turned to close it. As it closed he turned and looked down the street and glimpsed Jack Allinson dictating into his portable machine. Beside him were two men in suits, one of whom was staring through a theodolite. Alan dismissed the scene because he had more than enough on his mind. He unlocked the door of his council house at the Glebe, took off his coat, and slumped into the chair.

He declined his wife's kind offer of a sandwich, for he was not at all hungry. He felt physically sick. He sighed, and stretched out in his armchair beside an electric fire, his slippered feet on a footstool. The death of Mrs Jones had devastated him. He had known her through all the years of his life and he bathed in the waves of sorrow which flooded over him. With each new wave of emotion came a flood of memories so bright as to be real.

Sunday tea-times, when as a child he had always to be on best behaviour. The lace tablecloth, the smell of fresh ham, and the cake-stands full of cakes. And his mother, sitting beside her young friend Mrs Jones, talking of events at the chapel and among the village folk.

Sunday-school lessons, sitting on tiny wooden chairs, as Mrs Jones had told them the stories of Jesus, and he'd gazed at her sparkling blue eyes, and seen the conviction of faith there. Her lessons, so ordered, yet so full of life.

And her presence at all the most important moments of his life. The 'wedding breakfast' she provided in the chapel schoolroom after his wedding, a meal fit for a king. He saw her there smiling and laughing, and 'wishing them well'; so busy, so supportive and so kind.

Her solos had punctuated the years. They marked out the high points of life at the Wesleyans ... Sunday-school anniversaries when the children took part ... and chapel anniversaries ... and her beautiful clear voice ... 'All in the April evening ...'.

Tears were falling down Alan Drifford's cheeks. He'd never before stopped to think about what she'd meant to him, and he'd never bothered to thank her.

Darker memories now. The funeral of Mr Jones, nearly twenty years ago. What a disappointment her marriage had been; he was a regular at the Fox and Hounds, a drunk, a mean and spiteful man. Yet through all the years she'd been faithful to him, trying to keep the home together. Perhaps it was good that they'd never had children.

How strange, he thought, that Stan Menston should come to chapel again the week that Mrs Jones had died. His last visit had been for the funeral of Mr Jones, one of his most faithful regulars.

And then that still, cold hand. Outstretched, and open, pointing upward. As if she'd released her soul to the good Lord. Her time had come, and she had been ready to go.

'Drink this, love,' said Mrs Drifford, handing him a steaming cup of tea. She bent down and kissed his cheek, and her lips touched the salty tears. Alan Drifford had not only lost a mentor, but the mainstay of his life.

He carefully placed the saucer on the floor, and clasped the china cup between his hands. Its warmth comforted him. He sipped the hot tea, and with his eyes tightly shut, he could hear the sound of singing echoing down the years. It was an old hymn, they hadn't sung it at the chapel for many years, but the sound of many voices lifted his spirit and he felt the comfort of the words.

> When peace like a river attendeth my way
> When sorrows like sea billows roll ...
> Whatever my lot,

Thou hast taught me to know
It is well, it is well with my soul.

Alan Drifford had not known many religious experiences in his life. He had led an ordered, safe existence, with all emotion carefully controlled. But now, at last, he was open to something new. His commitment had been to the chapel and its people, but now, in this dark storm of despair, he reached out to God with a desperation he'd never known before. And as he opened his eyes, he thought he saw the person of Jesus, standing before him, waiting.

The vision was disturbed by his wife, creeping into the room with a blanket and a hot water bottle. She gently pressed the warm bottle to him, and tucked the blanket around him.

'There you are, love,' she whispered. 'You've had some nasty shocks this morning. Take it easy.'

'Annie,' he looked up at her with the expression of a little child, looking for reassurance, 'how will I know what to do without Mrs Jones?'

Mrs Drifford knelt beside him. This was a rare moment of tenderness between them. She gently stroked his hand and whispered, 'Don't worry, love, the Lord will show you, if you ask him.'

These short moments were a turning-point in Alan Drifford's life. Annie bent forward and softly kissed his cheek.

'Thanks, love,' he said, and as soon as he closed his eyes he fell into a deep refreshing sleep.

The funeral of Mrs Jones was a good one, as funerals go. The harvest goods had been cleared away, the plaster dust removed, and a temporary piece of plaster-board placed above the hole in the loft. News about the structural report on the chapel had been easy to suppress, for news of Mrs Jones' death had dominated everyone's conversation.

Geoff Notes was thankful that the days before the funeral had been free of rain. He felt sure that the warm October sun had dried out the roof and so he was prepared to take the risk of holding the funeral in the main sanctuary of the church.

Somehow Geoff felt that it would probably be the last occasion on which the building would be used. It was fitting that it should be for the funeral of Mrs Jones. Perhaps it marked the end of an era.

The short ceremony over, the four black-clad undertaker's men lifted the coffin shoulder high, and walked slowly towards the door. The coffin was preceded by Geoff Notes, and followed by the Driffords, the Selhurst family, and the Field sisters. The rest of the congregation followed on behind.

Mrs Drifford had organised a ham-sandwich tea in Mrs Jones' house for those who'd travelled a distance, and for close friends of the deceased. They sat in the lounge making polite conversation, and longing to depart.

At last, when they had all gone and Mrs Drifford was finishing the washing-up, Alan Drifford pulled open the writing bureau which Mrs Jones had prized so much. He sat on the antique chair in front of it and turned the key of the small drawer in front of him. He pulled out the Last Will and Testament of Mrs Prunella Jones.

He was the legally named executor of her estate, and now that the funeral was over, he felt it was proper to open the will. Nothing could have prepared him for the shock of what the will contained. He had been given no advance warning of its contents.

'I, the undersigned, Prunella Jones, bequeath my entire estate including all savings, investments, property and possessions to the Church Council of Gospel End Wesleyans.'

Alan Drifford let out a gasp of delight. For he knew that, including the cottage, Mrs Jones' estate amounted to over forty thousand pounds. She always had been committed to the chapel, but he hadn't expected everything to be left to the Gospel End Wesleyans. He read on.

'These assets are to be used for the local church's work in the promulgation of total abstinence.'

'Oh dear, oh dear,' muttered Alan Drifford to himself. Her lifelong commitment had been to the propagation of temperance, and the demise of teetotalism within the Wesleyan movement had caused her great anguish. She obviously hoped that the money would save other local men from going the same drunken way as her departed husband, Harold Jones. Like many others before her, Prunella Jones intended to use her last will and testament to make one final statement from beyond the grave.

Alan Drifford folded up the will and carefully placed it back in the drawer. 'If only ... ' he whispered. If only she'd died after his meeting with the builder she might have changed her will and used the money to save Gospel End Wesleyan Chapel.

Chapter Five

The Signs

Sarah Notes and Jenny Drifford continued to see each other regularly, and the catastrophic events at the harvest seemed to strengthen their common view of things. Their friendship blossomed, and it seemed that each saw the relationship as a means of survival at Gospel End.

Sarah's interest in Green issues grew with each meeting, and within a matter of weeks she had read and digested Jenny's complete library of Green paperbacks. Conversation at their weekly coffee evenings revolved around ozone, acid rain, whales, seals, nuclear power, grain mountains, animal rights and an ever-growing agenda of other ecological causes.

Sarah was still unable to find a job in the locality and her growing fascination with Green issues was the only intellectual stimulus available to her. Geoff's preoccupation with the problems at Gospel End Wesleyans left her with a great deal of spare time on her hands, so she became more and more engrossed in her study of ecology and committed to a personal crusade to change the world.

Although a committed 'Green', Jenny's career took up most of her time, and she didn't have the energy to carry her intellectual commitment into action. She felt challenged by Sarah's growing commitment, and began to see that she would soon have to turn good intentions into practical action herself.

'It's no good,' Sarah concluded, sipping her decaffeinated 'Cambodian workers' coffee from a clumsy pottery mug, 'we've got to motivate the people of Gospel End to look at their lifestyle, and we must begin to challenge some of these farmers about the wasteful methods they're using.'

Jenny Drifford made no reply. As a child of Gospel End she could see the implications of Sarah's idea. She knew that any crusade to change Gospel End could end in heartbreak and tears. She also knew that her new friend was in deadly earnest, and that with or without her support Sarah had already decided on action.

Geoff had noted the change in Sarah with growing concern. It had all started innocently enough when he had remarked that the new 'Earth-Friendly' washing-up liquid didn't seem to give a good lather. Then came the cheaply-packaged third-world coffee and tea which didn't seem to have the richness of taste of Geoff's favourite blends. He also noticed that the house was getting colder as the heating system was administered by Sarah with miserly efficiency.

Gradually the eating habits of the Notes family were revolutionised. Soya beans replaced pork sausages, and some rather watery rice dishes replaced Geoff's favourite meals. He found that he was leaving the table with his appetite unsatisfied.

The notice in the window of Field's grocery store was the last straw. In bold coloured lettering it proclaimed 'SAVE THE EARTH BEFORE IT'S TOO LATE ... FIRST MEETING OF GOSPEL END ACTION GROUP, THE MANSE, WEDNESDAY, 7.30pm. Further details from Sarah Notes at the manse.'

'What on earth are you doing, Sarah?' Geoff protested, as he struggled to eat the vegetarian dish before him. 'You might at least have told me about this meeting, rather than let me see it advertised in the shop window.'

'But, darling,' Sarah sympathised, 'you're so busy at the moment that I didn't want to bother you. There's nothing to it really, it's just that Jenny and I feel we ought to see if there are any others who feel like us ... we need to translate Green concerns into practical action at Gospel End.'

Geoff sighed. 'Look, darling,' – he was choosing his words carefully – 'heaven knows these Green issues are important, but I think it's easy to get things out of perspective. I'd hate you, well, er ... to become extreme.'

'Extreme?' Sarah was really annoyed. 'The Green movement is one of the most important things happening in our culture today ... but the majority of the folk at Gospel End Wesleyans don't even seem to have heard of it! I don't interfere with your ministry at the church, and I don't expect you to interfere with this. In fact, I had hoped you might even come along to the meeting.'

Geoff flicked through his diary. There was a church committee in the neighbouring village which he simply had to attend. The committee, on the restructuring of Methodist committees, was the kind of event which ministers were supposed to attend. If he was absent his superiors in the clerical hierarchy would undoubtedly note his disinterest.

'I can't come on Wednesday; maybe some other time,' he said sharply. He snapped his diary shut, and chewed the watery rice. He dreamed of mixed grills, lamb chops and shepherd's pie.

'Sarah, I just can't survive on this stuff.' He tipped a forkful of the rice back onto the plate, his voice harsh and uncompromising. 'It may be healthy and ecologically sound but I just don't like it ... and with the hours I'm working at the moment I need to eat.'

'Oh, come on, Geoff, it's not that bad,' she said firmly.

He snatched the plate and poured the meal into the kitchen bin. 'It's rubbish, you're just being stupid.' He was furious.

Sarah ran upstairs and curled up in the bed. She pulled the covers over her head and heard Geoff's angry voice still ringing in her ears. The front door slammed shut as Geoff went out to his evening meeting. The pressures of recent weeks were beginning to tell on both of them.

Sarah lay in the darkened room for some time, feeling at an all-time low. She was only surviving at

Gospel End because of Jenny's friendship and the stimulus of her 'Green' reading. She'd never seen Geoff so angry; he was usually such a placid person, and there was a hardness in his eyes which frightened her.

She was hurt that Geoff didn't approve of the meals, and angry that he considered the reorganisation committee more important than her Action Group; but more importantly, she felt they were drifting apart.

At last she sat up in the bed, pulled her address book out of her bedside drawer, went downstairs to Geoff's untidy study, and dialled a number on the antiquated phone. Her conversation with Janet Winter lasted for nearly an hour, but any thought of the escalating phone bill was far from her mind. She desperately needed to talk to someone outside the situation, and she trusted Janet completely.

The warm and friendly voice of Janet in Shetland was reassuring, and it was strangely comforting for Sarah to hear Janet describe some of the problems which she had faced in recent weeks as a new minister in a strange environment. In a gentle and loving way, Janet reminded Sarah of the night they both prayed in the college chapel, and of Sarah's new-found faith and growing love for Geoff. She gently suggested that perhaps Sarah needed to weigh her priorities again.

Sarah felt embarrassed when Janet began to pray for her over the phone, because it seemed such a strange thing to do. But it was such a beautiful prayer, so naturally spoken, that Sarah felt a wave of healing love flowing over her. As she put down the receiver, she noticed that there, in the middle of Geoff's overflowing desk, was the candle which Janet had given her. The holder was already covered in dust.

The harvest catastrophe had happened on a Sunday, Mrs Jones died on the Monday, and her funeral was on the Friday. On Saturday morning Alan Drifford nailed a large sign to the front door of the church. It quickly became an important talking point. The bold red lettering on the white board was blunt. 'DANGER: chapel premises unsafe. DO NOT ENTER.'

Normally church building projects move exceedingly slowly, but this was a situation where all involved felt the need to do something quickly. The premises were completely unusable, a state of affairs which rang alarm bells in the corridors of church administration. The phones had been buzzing all week, and a hastily convened 'Property Commission' was scheduled for that Saturday morning. Jack Allinson loaned Geoff six white hard hats which were distributed among all visiting officials for their own protection.

The six consisted of a surveyor, an insurance assessor, and church officials of varying status and authority, some of whom had travelled from the other end of the country to view the hole in the ceiling and the wet rot in the loft. After their two-hour inspection they agreed to prepare separate reports and meet again the following week. Geoff was asked to ascertain from the District Council what plans for redevelopment were scheduled for Gospel End, and whether any help might be forth coming towards the reconstruction of Gospel End Wesleyans.

Another sign in the window of Field's grocery store was also creating considerable interest within the community. Beside Sarah's colourful poster was a very plain sheet of paper with a biro-inscribed message which read, 'Due to problems with the chapel building, services will be held in the Junior School on a temporary basis.' The words 'temporary basis' were underlined.

The headmistress at the Junior School, Mrs Frederickson, had been most helpful and co-operative. She told Geoff Notes, who was seated in the very low easy chair in her office, that she had had chapel links in the past, but had not attended worship for many years. The Gospel End Wesleyans could have the school hall for a modest rent, but she felt it incumbent upon herself to warn Geoff Notes about Bill Mann, the caretaker.

'It's rather embarrassing, Mr Notes,' she said softly, as she leaned across her large desk and peered down at the young minister in the low chair. 'Sometimes I don't feel as though I'm in charge here at all, I feel as though he is!' She tossed back her head in the direction of the caretaker's cottage at the other end of the children's playground.

'He's not very co-operative, I'm afraid. He's very influential in the union, too. The slightest problem seems to get blown out of all proportion, and the next thing I know is that I have the Director of Education on the line. So, Mr Notes, you can have the school every Sunday as far as I'm concerned – as long as it's all right with Bill Mann.'

Unfortunately, Geoff Notes' meeting with Bill was not quite so successful. Bill was the kind of wizened little man who seemed to relish discord, and who saw every situation as a potential problem. Alarm bells were always ringing in his head, and he liked to use the word 'no' more regularly than the word 'yes'. If there are such people as 'yes men', then Bill was undoubtedly a 'no man'.

'It's like this,' Bill moaned to Geoff as he leaned on his broom in the playground. 'I consider Sunday as my day off. I work jolly hard all week, and I leave everything straight on Friday afternoon. There's no way I can clean up after you lot in time for Monday morning.'

Geoff grinned appeasingly, but in his mind he was trying to imagine what Bill meant by 'clean up after you lot'. Perhaps Bill imagined that Gospel End Wesleyans were some kind of leather-jacketed motorcycle gang who wanted to service their bikes in the school classrooms before riding them around the school hall. Geoff pulled himself back to reality.

'We're really not a very messy lot, you know, Mr Mann, and we'd be delighted to clean up after ourselves,' Geoff said reassuringly. 'We really are in dire straights, and we need your help.'

Bill looked the young parson straight in the eye. He was used to standing up to officialdom. 'Very well, then,' said Bill, 'but this can only be a temporary arrangement, and I will be constantly reviewing the situation on a day-to-day basis.' Gospel End

Wesleyans would worship at the school, but the words 'temporary basis' were acknowledged by all.

Geoff Notes had done his best to make the school a sanctuary. John Selhurst had helped him to transport the lectern, communion table, and the two ornately carved communion chairs to the school on the tractor-trailer. Geoff had ferried hymn books, hymn board, communion glasses, altar-falls and other paraphernalia in the boot of his car.

Of all the changes, however, perhaps the Sunday service itself was the most disturbing and controversial. Geoff Notes had prayerfully planned the service, and seen the move from chapel to school as the opportunity to introduce many of the new ideas which he felt could revolutionise worship at Gospel End Wesleyans.

First, he put out only as many chairs as he estimated the number of worshippers to be. He set a total of forty-six in place; but they were not in rows – they were in a tight semi-circle. Geoff's training in group dynamics convinced him that this would help to create a much greater sense of belonging and fellowship, and could be the key to services really 'taking off'.

Next, he had purchased out of his own limited income some fifty copies of a new song book entitled *Freely, freely*. Rather ironic, he thought, as this purchase had nearly bankrupted him.

Sarah, partly in appeasement for having organised the Action Group, had agreed to accompany the new songs on guitar and pressed Jenny into playing her long-disused flute. There was no way that Miss Field the younger – who had been church organist for over thirty years – could handle this 'new stuff' as she called it.

Steven Jones stood at the door of the school hall with a pile of hymn books and *Freely, freelies,* and as skilfully as a juggler managed to shake each worshipper's hand as well as giving them the two very different hymn books and a sheet of church notices.

He was just as surprised as the previous week when, at one minute before service time, Stan and Molly Menston entered. But this time they did not come in with cowering unease, they strode in confidently and wished Steven a hearty 'Good morning'.

Many of the worshippers who entered were faced with a complex puzzle as they gazed at the layout of chairs in the school hall. Where would they sit? Many of the congregation had occupied the same pew and the same seat within that pew for decades. Faced with a semi-circle of two rows, how could they juxtaposition themselves into basically the same pattern as before?

They all did their best. Those who normally sat on the left continued to do so, and those on the right found space there. But they all traditionally sat near the back, so the second row filled up quickly, leaving embarrassed latecomers to occupy the seats in the front row, where they fidgeted uncomfortably.

Geoff Notes had placed the lectern in the centre of the semi-circle, as he felt that an 'in the round' approach might enable him to relate to the congregation more informally.

The move from fixed pews, high pulpit and church organ to worship in the round with piano, guitar and flute was probably the most dramatic revolution in worship at Gospel End Wesleyans in all its history. Geoff had even decided to do without his cassock and adopt the 'lounge-suit approach' much advocated by some of his more revolutionary college friends.

Although Geoff's style was still quite dignified he was much more relaxed than previously. From his opening, 'Good morning friends, and welcome to worship' through to his suggestion that 'you might like to clap your hands during this next song', he was obviously trying a completely new approach. It didn't surprise him, however, that no one accepted the invitation to 'put down your *Freely, freelies* and put your hands together'.

It would be wrong to say that everyone hated the new style. Farmer Selhurst Junior appreciated the new approach, and if others had done so he would willingly have 'put his hands together'. Even some of the older ladies appreciated Geoff's more informal style: it made worship somehow friendlier and more relaxed. But there were others, like Alan Drifford, who in their anger and distress could barely remain in their seats for the duration of the service.

But Stan and Molly Menston were obviously in their element. This informal 'sing-along' approach was reminiscent of Saturday nights at the pub; and they liked the new songs accompanied by Sarah and Jenny. Stan even found himself swaying to

'Bind us together', and he beamed at Geoff when the young parson made humorous remarks in the introduction to his sermon.

'I'm told that when the first Wesleyan preachers came to Gospel End the local folk put them in the stocks and threw things at them! I just hope you're not going to do the same to me!' Humour, Geoff realised, was one way of getting under people's guard ... and he was certainly facing a very guarded congregation that morning!

Geoff's text was a simple one, 'Simon Peter, do you love me?' He read it, and paused. Clutching the lectern he drew himself up to his full height, and launched into his message with abandon.

'This has been one of the most traumatic weeks we've ever known at Gospel End Wesleyans. The ruined Harvest Festival, the declaration that our premises are unsafe, and the death of one whose whole life was given over to this church have shaken us all to the core. But sometimes it takes a series of events such as these to bring us back to basics ... and to make us ask ... why is there a Gospel End Wesleyans, anyway?'

This was powerful stuff, delivered with passion and conviction. Even Alan Drifford was on the edge of his seat. 'Maybe we'll never move back into our premises again' – there was an audible groan from many of the congregation – 'maybe things will never be the same again. But this needn't be an hour of disaster, but an hour of opportunity. Perhaps it's time for us all to hear Christ's challenging call. Do you love *me*, do you love *me*? Not the chapel, not the tradition, not the denomination, not the fellowship ... but Christ himself.'

Geoff, feeling more confident, let go of the lectern, and began to walk to and fro within the semicircle. He found the words flowing easily, and even his voice had dropped its parsonical tone.

'I don't know what the future holds for us as a church in this village; but I do know that Christ is alive and that it is our duty to share his love with all we meet. We can stand and gaze longingly at the past, or we can rediscover a fresh love for the Saviour, and move forward with him to become the church he wants us to be. But before we can do that we all need to come back to basics. Christ is asking you this morning, "Do you love me?" Will you respond?'

Geoff paused, and surveyed his hearers. The blank faces he had looked down on in previous weeks were gone. The people were really listening, and their eyes showed it. Sarah's eyes were wide open with admiration; Mr Selhurst Senior had heard echoes of a message heard once, long before, and was leaning forward in earnest concentration; Stan was beaming approvingly ... and there, sitting alone on a chair behind the second row, Alan Drifford was wiping tears from his eyes.

For Alan Drifford the timing of this message was perfect. His chapel ruined, his mentor dead, his prejudices about worship awakened ... he felt that perhaps his vision of Jesus and Geoff's sermon were somehow linked. Perhaps God was trying to tell him something.

Chapter Six

Shocking News

Geoff Notes drove up the long and winding farm track towards the Selhursts' farmhouse. Apart from a very brief call to introduce himself when he first arrived in the village, he'd never given the Selhursts a proper pastoral visit.

As he got out of his car he saw the shadowy figure of Brian Selhurst in the milking parlour, and he paused to watch him filling the feeding troughs with hay. Geoff took a deep breath as he entered the milking parlour, and sneezed as his nostrils filled with the coarse fumes of disinfectant. Brian Selhurst looked up in surprise.

'Good morning, Brian,' beamed Geoff. 'I thought I'd just call round to see how things are.'

'Ah, Mr Notes, I was just thinking about you,' the old farmer retorted. He did not return Geoff's beam of greeting but gave him something more akin to a scowl. Before Geoff could reply the old man had launched into a prepared speech, which he delivered slowly and ponderously in a broad Yorkshire accent. Brian Selhurst was not the kind of man to be interrupted.

'That was a good sermon you gave on Sunday, but I didn't reckon much to the rest of it. I've been going to that chapel for most of my life and I've never been to such an awful service – to put it politely, it was a disgrace, Mr Notes. It just wasn't dignified, and I didn't like it. If that's the sort of thing you're going to be offering us from now on, I'll be forced to take my membership elsewhere.'

Geoff made no reply. Emotionally, he felt as though he'd just fallen from a high building. He looked down at the pools of disinfectant on the concrete floor and his self-confidence evaporated.

'I'm sorry you feel like that, Brian. I really didn't intend to upset you, and I hope you'll reconsider your decision – but I'm afraid worship has got to change if the church is to have any meaning to this community.'

'You may feel it's time for worship to change, but that's not how I feel,' the farmer drawled as he wagged his finger aggressively. 'I've been going to that chapel for over sixty years, and I don't see that anything needs changing. The faster we can put the old chapel back in order and get back to normal the happier I'll be. You can ask my wife, she says the same.'

Geoff Notes looked up at the old man's face, angered by his obstinacy. 'I think that's wishful thinking, Brian. That chapel is quite beyond repair, and when the Commission meets next

Saturday I expect they'll be asking for its immediate demolition in the interests of public safety. We've all got to face up to the challenge. It's not going to be easy for any of us.'

Brian Selhurst was unable to respond, for the thought of the chapel's demise was too much for him to bear. He picked up his dusty cloth cap, swept back his greying hair, and pulled it firmly on. 'I'll be seeing you, then,' he said, as he strode back to the farmhouse with his hands in his overall pockets. Brian Selhurst never had been able to resolve situations of conflict.

The visit over, Geoff Notes strode back to his car. The quicker he could get out of that farmyard the happier he'd feel. But that was not to be. He twisted the ignition key again and again, but nothing happened because the starter motor had jammed. This had to be the worst of all moments in which to break down. Geoff sat back and sighed and, just as he did so, a tractor swept round the corner and into the yard. John Selhurst was back from drilling the fields.

Geoff got out of the car with desperation written all over his face. 'Hello, John, any chance of a spot of help?'

The young farmer ambled confidently towards him. 'What's the problem, Mr Notes?' Within a matter of minutes the bonnet was open, and John Selhurst was straining and heaving to release the jammed starter motor with a spanner.

'That was a nice service on Sunday, Mr Notes. I liked them new songs out of *Freely, freely*. If services are going to be more like that you'll be seeing more of me on a Sunday. It made me feel right good. I've been whistling them tunes all week.'

'That's not how your dad feels about it all, John,' Geoff murmured apologetically.

'You don't want to worry about him,' John smiled, emerging from under the bonnet. 'He'll come round, just give him time.'

The starter motor was not repairable, at least not by John Selhurst, so Geoff was coerced into being towed to the garage behind John's Land Rover. Within a matter of minutes Geoff found himself clutching his steering wheel grimly as he flew along behind the Land Rover, his car bouncing over the farmyard track like a ship in a thunderstorm. He saw it as a parable of his own ministry at Gospel End Wesleyans ... a rough ride completely outside his own control. He clutched the wheel and hoped beyond hope that God was in the driving seat.

Once the car had been safely deposited at Gospel End garage, a dilapidated structure with the general ambience of a motor museum, John Selhurst took Geoff back to the manse in the Land Rover and was persuaded to stay for a cup of tea.

'This tea's a bit weak,' said John, as he stirred a third spoonful of sugar into it. The two men were seated in the kitchen of the manse, and Sarah was standing by the cooker mixing ingredients into a bowl.

'It's Cambodian workers' tea,' said Sarah, turning from the cooker and smiling at him. 'It may not taste so good, but it makes an important political point – and all the profits go towards relief projects in Cambodia.'

'I like a cup of tea that you can stand your spoon up in,' said John, pulling a face each time he sipped from the pottery mug. 'We like Yorkshire tea round here!'

The exchange was good-natured, and Geoff could see that John Selhurst was far more open to new ideas than his father.

'What's this meeting you're organising about saving the world, then?' John asked, a twinkle of humour in his eye.

'It's just that Jenny Drifford and I feel that something should be *done* about Green issues in our village, rather than just talking about it all. And as a farmer, John, you should be specially concerned. Why don't you come?'

'Aye, all right then. I'll see you on Wednesday.'

Sarah and Geoff looked at each other in amazement. Neither had expected this kind of interest from a member of the farming community.

'Would you like another cup of tea before you go?' Sarah asked politely. 'I could add a couple of extra tea-bags to improve the taste!'

'No, thanks,' said John, 'I got the point with one tea-bag!' And bidding everyone the customary Selhurst, 'I'll be seeing you, then,' he left.

Geoff watched the Land Rover disappear into the distance and closed the manse door; it was barely five thirty pm and already dark. Sarah was still stirring ingredients into a delicious steaming chicken casserole as Geoff stood behind her and gave her an affectionate squeeze. He looked over her shoulder and smiled. He hadn't seen such an appetising meal for weeks.

'I'm coming to the meeting on Wednesday, too,' he told her. 'I reckon I can give the committee reorganisation committee a miss for once. I'd like to know more about Green issues and study them from a Christian perspective.'

Sarah smiled. 'Thanks, darling, I hoped you'd change your mind. I've been worried sick about that meeting ever since I put the poster up. Would you help me lead it?' He held her tight and whispered, 'Yes.'

She stopped stirring the casserole, turned, and kissed his cheek. 'I do love you,' she whispered. They kissed a soft kiss of reconciliation. Perhaps, Geoff mused, it hadn't been such a bad day after all.

The Action Group meeting was much better attended than either Sarah or Jenny had dared to hope. What fascinated Geoff was that each of the twelve who sat in the large lounge of the manse were closely associated with Gospel End Wesleyans in some way. Perhaps, Geoff reasoned, they had come because the meeting was being held at the manse, or maybe because the Wesleyans had a sharpened social conscience. Whatever their reason for attending the meeting, however, he was thrilled to see that so many of his flock were concerned about world issues. He was relieved that he hadn't missed it.

There was a lively buzz of conversation as they sat and drank their Cambodian coffee. There were several young wives seated on the floor, Mrs Frederickson the headmistress was perched on a high-backed wooden chair, while Steve Jenkins and John Selhurst sat in a corner in deep conversation. Just before the meeting started Alan Drifford and his wife walked in. They'd come to support Jenny.

It was quite the strangest meeting that Geoff Notes had ever chaired. As it was not an official church meeting there was no prayer at the beginning, no reading from the Scriptures, no carefully prepared agenda emanating from Head Office — yet it was undoubtedly a Christian meeting.

As different members of the group pooled their concerns about the world, the conversation gradually became more personal. They shared their guilt regarding the third world, they talked about their struggle to know which ozone-friendly products to buy, and they aired their fears for the future.

It was one of those meetings when each contribution built on the previous speaker's words, and there was a commonality of feeling among the group that Geoff had never seen in a Gospel End Wesleyans meeting before. What astonished him even more was that God was getting more mention here than in any discussion he'd previously witnessed in the church schoolroom. It was as though the local Christians, set free from discussing the guttering and roofing of their chapel, were at last released to share the deep things which really bothered them.

'What disturbs me most about the Green movement,' said Geoff, 'is that it often seems to have become a religion in its own right. The earth is the new god, and the only hope is in man. As a Christian I believe that the earth is God's creation, and that the only hope is in changing men and women through the power of the risen Christ.'

Even Mrs Frederickson, whose attendance at chapel over the last twenty years had become less and less frequent, talked about the Creator God. Geoff would never have guessed that she was a secret believer from his brief encounter with her at the school. It was clear that Mrs Frederickson, though not a 'regular' at the chapel, had a real experience of God.

Alan Drifford didn't speak, but his eyes betrayed a real and intense interest in all that was being said. He hadn't been to such a happy and lively meeting at the chapel for many years; and he felt he wanted to be a part of this group who were 'out to change the world'.

Sarah was ebulliently happy. She found it hard to believe that the vibrant conversation was flowing from the same dowdy, depressing group of people whom she'd seen sitting in the pews Sunday by Sunday. There was a kind of energy and excitement among the group which she hadn't experienced since her university days. Perhaps, after all, there was a place for her at Gospel End Wesleyans!

Jenny Drifford was happy, too. Not because of the discussion on Green issues, not because of the vibrant conversation, and not even because her opinions were sought and valued. Jenny Drifford had become aware that the young farmer, John Selhurst, was looking at her with special tenderness … and she found her eyes being drawn towards his again and again throughout the evening. It was little wonder, then, that after everyone else had gone that John and Jenny offered to do the washing up; and that Geoff and Sarah retired to their lounge because the two at the kitchen sink were obviously so engrossed in conversation, and so evidently wanting space to be alone.

'It was a good meeting tonight, Sarah,' Geoff beamed. 'It's the first meeting I've chaired and not felt drained afterwards! I hope you didn't mind me saying that prayer at the end, but it just seemed right, somehow.'

'It was right, Geoff, and I'm glad you prayed,' said Sarah, curling up on the settee beside him. 'I enjoyed the meeting, it felt like a church should feel ... and I believe that Jesus would have felt at home with us here tonight.'

Jenny poked her head around the door. 'John and I are off now, he's going to drive me home.'

'Goodnight,' all four chimed in unison. Geoff smiled at Sarah, and though neither spoke they both remembered their first meeting at the rag week bed push in a distant life long ago, when they were both students at Bristol.

The Council offices at Great Orton were housed in a beautiful old country mansion surrounded by Portakabins. The planning department would not have permitted such a strange mix of buildings to exist anywhere else, but the Council looked after its own.

Geoff sat on an old wooden bench in the magnificent oak panelled hall until the receptionist authorised him to climb the broad stone staircase and knock on the large door marked 'Mr Smythe:

Town Planning Executive'. He was impressed that he had been granted an audience with the big chief. He had expected some junior clerk to answer the Building Commission's questions about future plans for Gospel End.

'Sit down, Mr Notes ... would you like coffee?' Geoff took a seat at a long polished table where a pile of plans lay partly unfurled. The rich aroma of freshly percolated coffee emanating from the corner of the office was too much for him to resist. Geoff sipped the coffee, and savoured its rich flavour. The Cambodian blend still had a long way to go! The Council official sat in a chair opposite and they eyed each other suspiciously over the shiny oak surface. Geoff felt that this pin-striped-suited gentleman was too pleasant to be genuine.

'How did you know about the new plans for Gospel End, Mr Notes? We have been very careful about security on this matter.'

Geoff Notes sipped his coffee. He knew instantly that he was close to discovering something vital, so he decided to bluff the official into revealing more.

'I have come here to ask you to come clean, and tell the local people everything. They should be consulted from the earliest stages of any new project.' Geoff always had been good at role play, and he looked every inch the angry young man.

'Very well,' sighed the official, 'but I must ask you to treat the information I am going to give you sensitively – the plans which I am going to show you are, to say the least, political dynamite.'

The official took the pile of plans and rolled them out in front of the wide-eyed young minister.

The two men spread out their palms on the paper to prevent the plans from furling at the edges. Geoff gasped as he saw the title. 'Gospel End: New Town Proposal: HM Government.' Before him were hundreds of little shaded rectangles, which he took to be houses.

'Within the next few years,' the official declared, 'Gospel End will increase by twenty thousand people. A new industrial complex will be built there to service the micro-chip industry, and we will be putting in a new infrastructure to service the local area including schools, health centres, supermarkets, roads – the lot. It's going to be a big job.'

'And what about the local people? They've lived there for generations, the whole place is steeped in history. You can't just bulldoze it all away.' Geoff was just getting into his stride.

'You misjudge me, Mr Notes. We will be doing all in our power to keep the village architecture intact, and we'll be blending the new estates into the four valleys around Gospel End. We'll obviously be making a feature of the river, the pub and ... perhaps most important of all, the chapel. We'll be putting a Preservation Order on it shortly.'

Geoff Notes was flabbergasted. He barely knew what to say, or how to say it, yet he managed to retain a professional pose by looking at the plans in front of him as if he understood them.

'We'll be going public with this on Friday, and of course there will be six months of detailed public consultation before we begin work. But, bearing in mind the current political climate within the

Council here, it's only really a matter of courtesy. You can rest assured, Mr Notes, that you'll have many more souls to care for in the coming few years – some of them American and Japanese!'

Geoff Notes and the official opposite lifted their palms off the plan, and it curled immediately. Geoff was too stunned to think of anything worthwhile to say, so they exchanged courteous 'Good mornings', and he descended the broad staircase. His mind was reeling under the implications of the Council's plan for Gospel End.

Chapter Seven

No Turning Back

The news about the Council's development plans for Gospel End filled the front page and centrefold of the *Orton Courier* the following Friday. There were detailed plans of the scheme, and a group photograph featuring the planning executive, Mr Smythe, and three Japanese businessmen who were beaming from ear to ear.

The inhabitants at Gospel End reacted to the article with total disbelief. They whispered about it to Mrs Field at the post-office counter, who had a copy of the centrefold conveniently spread out in front of her.

'They can't do that to our village,' whispered Miss Field to her sister-in-law, as she collected her pension. 'They'd never get away with it. I mean, there'd be a public outcry.'

'Well, you never know,' replied the postmistress from behind the counter, 'if the Council really want it, they might push it through. It would be a tragedy.' But even as she spoke she pictured a new Field's superstore with rows of shopping trolleys outside the door. She always had been ambitious for her husband's business.

The teachers in the staff-room at Gospel End Junior School gathered round the outspread centrefold during morning playtime. They were using a ruler to work out the size of the rectangle marked 'new school', so that they could deduce the area of the new premises. They all seemed rather rusty in the art of converting centimetres into square metres.

'The village will be completely spoiled,' stated Mrs Frederickson, while imagining her pristine new school, its survival now secure for ever.

Alan Drifford and his wife had the plan spread out on the dining room table and were sharing a large reading glass in order to read the tiny inscriptions beneath each rectangle.

'Well, at least one thing's certain,' smiled Alan Drifford, 'the chapel is secure. That's not moved — in fact, with that Preservation Order on it there's no chance that it'll ever be pulled down.' Even as he spoke he imagined the Gospel End Wesleyan Chapel standing strong and tall amidst a sea of new buildings. The mental image disturbed him, but he didn't really know why.

Over at the Fox and Hounds Stan Menston was leaning over the bar and making a speech. 'Of course, they'll never get away with it. It's another of those crackpot schemes that'll come to nothing.' There was an uncanny silence as they drank their beer in the Fox and Hounds that night, and imagined the snug filled with smiling Japanese businessmen drinking cocktails.

The Selhursts, in their farmhouse kitchen, were looking at the plans outstretched on the kitchen table in disbelief. Neither John, nor his mother or father, had spoken for some time. They just stood and gazed. Their farmhouse was clearly drawn but the track was now a new link road, and their fields were filled with 'a mix of starter homes, maisonettes, and mews-style executive houses'.

'Over my dead body,' whispered Brian Selhurst. And he meant it.

The following morning was Saturday, and the six members of the Church Property Commission got their chance to comment on the new town plan. They all sat around the vestry table with their hard white hats firmly on their heads. Geoff saw the funny side of every situation, and wondered if hard hats might catch on as a new form of clerical attire especially suitable for church council meetings.

All six looked down in silence at the plans outspread in front of them.

'It looks like a very nice development,' said the Commission's architect. 'It's got a lot of imaginative touches – I particularly like the mix of house-styles and the retention of the old community focus.'

'Rubbish,' thundered the dynamic young convenor who had travelled from London and who was high up in property affairs. 'They are using our chapel as a museum piece to give this concrete shopping complex some character and they'll make us pay for it.' Everyone, including Geoff Notes and the architect, murmured approval. It's quite amazing, thought Geoff, how in church committees the most important official present can demolish everyone else's arguments at a stroke. Even the architect, whose fees were payable by the Head Office, quickly changed sides.

'Yes, you've got a good point there. In the current economic climate we're unlikely to get any help with renovation ... and by being so prominent in the town plan we'll be responsible for keeping this place up for ever.'

'If you want to demolish,' Geoff interposed helpfully, 'you'll have to move quickly. Mr Smythe, the Planning Executive, told me that they'd be putting a Preservation Order on the building quite soon.'

The other members of the commission looked at each other with horror. The words 'Preservation Order' struck terror into the very heart of Head Office bureaucracy. They already had eight hundred buildings with Preservation Orders on them—eight hundred buildings of 'special architectural interest', eight hundred buildings that were costing them a fortune.

The convenor, half hoping to catch the next train back to London, put some papers in his briefcase and snapped it shut. 'Well, that clinches it for me. I propose that Gospel End Wesleyans be demolished forthwith in the interests of public safety, and that we set up a commission to investigate the possibilities of rebuilding on the site as soon as possible. Are we all agreed?'

'Shouldn't we consult the local folk first?' asked Geoff, nervously. 'Some of them are going to be very upset.'

'Yes,' sighed the official, 'but the word is "inform", not "consult". If you start consulting them we'll have a petition and a march to headquarters organised, and none of us wants that. Simply explain that we've not the money to keep this place going, and that it's dangerous. Tell them tomorrow – and it'll be down by Friday. Now, gentlemen, are we agreed?'

'Agreed.'

The London official disappeared through the door, and was driven off at great speed. He might just make that train back to London.

Sunday morning worship in the Junior School followed much the same pattern as the previous week: Miss Fields at the piano, with choruses from *Freely, freely* accompanied by various instruments. Sarah's little band had more than doubled in size – they now had a recorder, violin and another guitar.

Extra chairs had to be brought in because there were sixty worshippers rather than the predicted forty-six. A crisis in a village community always brings out the lapsed. The service concluded with an 'extraordinary church meeting', which was chaired by Geoff. This time there was no previously prepared agenda handed over by Alan Drifford, and no secret meetings to fix the business up at the late Mrs Jones' house. Although it had been a long service because Geoff's new style of worship tended to stretch things to ninety minutes rather than the traditional hour, everyone stayed for the meeting.

'My friends,' Geoff began warmly, 'I appreciate your willingness to stay behind for this meeting. I know that this is most irregular, but we are living in unusual days here at Gospel End. As you know, the Head Office Property Commission sat at Gospel End yesterday in emergency session. They have examined detailed structural reports of the Wesleyan chapel and decided that it is a dangerous and unsafe structure, and that to repair it is just not viable. They have decided, as legal owners of the property, to demolish it this week.'

The whole meeting groaned in disapproval. 'They don't know what they're talking about,' shouted Brian Selhurst. John called, 'Hear, hear,' and there were murmurs all over the room of 'It's ridiculous,' and 'Who do they think they are?'

Geoff began to feel very nervous. He leaned on the table for support. It was all very well for London officials to make announcements, but none of the hard-hatted brigade were here with him now when he really needed them.

'Please, friends, please.' Geoff hoped that he might yet be able to convince them. 'It would cost hundreds of thousands of pounds to put that place in order, and I for one think that it would be money wasted. A church is people, not a building ... and if we were set free from the building, perhaps we could discover what our new role should be in the proposed new town.'

Geoff had lit the blue touch-paper, and he sat down. The explosion was immediate. From then on he didn't chair the meeting; it would have been impossible – even if he'd wanted to.

'Mr Chairman, I protest!' shouted Brian Selhurst. 'This chapel has stood here for more than a century. We've worshipped in it week in, week out, and it's ours. Some jumped-up little committee from Head Office can't just walk in and decide ... it's just not fair. And as for this new town, it's just a pipe dream ... it'll never happen, not over my dead body.'

Steve Jenkins found himself shaking with anger, and he was desperately trying to control what he said. 'As a member of the Property Committee I know that there are real problems with that building. It will be an expensive business. But we've tackled big problems before ... I'm sure that Head Office will come up with some grants to help us again, if we make enough fuss.'

Miss Field junior, the church organist who had recently been demoted to church pianist, spoke in a shrill emotional voice which the congregation had never heard her use before. The use of the *Freely, freelies* and the growing 'worship band' had wound her up during the service, but the demolition of the chapel was the last straw.

'No one here has mentioned the organ. As you know, it's a fine instrument, and has accompanied our singing for over eighty years. Are you proposing to demolish that, too, Mr Notes? It is quite, quite ridiculous. Ever since you arrived here, we've had nothing but problems ... I really wonder if you don't rather enjoy the thought of demolishing all that's most precious to us. Well, I, for one, have had enough ... '

She was like an express train racing down a track

and there was no way of stopping her or turning her back.

'The Wesleyan chapel, the organ, the singing ... these things are everything to me ... and you just come in here and ruin everything. Well, I resign. You'll have to find yourself another organist.' And with that, she stormed out. The meeting was silenced. Her sister walked out to comfort her. The sound of sobbing seeped in from the school corridor outside.

Jenny Drifford flicked back the wave of fair hair which curled over her forehead – she always sported the latest style – and stood confidently to make a speech. She was immaculately dressed in her purple business suit, and looked every inch the young female executive.

'Chair, may I speak as one who represents the future? I work in a highly competitive business environment. To put it bluntly, the kind of things which go on in church life would never be permitted in my company. Gospel End Wesleyan Chapel has no great architectural beauty to my thinking. It was put up nearly two centuries ago to cater for the farming families and their labourers who lived at Gospel End. It was designed as a preaching house, and it's totally unsuited to the needs of our new forms of worship. It sits here, year by year, like a great monument to the past. It appears off-putting and even frightening to many of the young people in this village. It's a hangover from the past and does the gospel of Jesus Christ no favours. And, if I may say so, it is the least energy-efficient building in the area. Every time we heat that place we say to the world 'We don't care about the environment.'

'That's rubbish,' thundered Brian Selhurst. 'Gospel End Wesleyans is a good chapel. It's the place where we belong. We've taken our kids to be baptised there, and we've wept for our loved ones at funerals there ... it goes back down the generations and you can't just pull it down.'

John Selhurst looked down at his feet. He knew that Jenny was right, but he was scared to say so. The meeting was silent again. The sobbing outside continued. One of the young wives went out to see if she could help.

Stan Menston stood up. He was wheezing nervously. 'Mr Chairman, I am not a member of this chapel ... but may I speak?'

'Of course, Stan. Tell us what's on your mind.'

Several of the members present looked decidedly uncomfortable. The thought of Stan Menston addressing the church council was akin to blasphemy.

'If the experts tell us that the chapel is not repairable, it's not repairable. And all the huffing and groaning that's going on here today won't make any difference either way, it's just a waste of breath. The demolition of the chapel is a tragedy, and I for one will shed a tear when it's down ... but last week Geoff preached about loving the Lord, and being willing to leave everything to follow him. Maybe he's asking us to leave the old chapel behind and if we do I'm sure that he'll tell us what to do next ... if we ask him.'

Stan Menston gazed out over the assembly, his hands outstretched. He looked every inch the Old

Testament prophet. After a long pause, he sat down.

At last John Selhurst found the courage of his convictions. 'Mr Menston is right. I don't want to spend the rest of my life raising money to keep a building up ... there's more important things for Christians to be doing. I like the chapel, of course I do, but there's more to being a Christian than keeping a chapel up. The Lord will show us, if we ask him.'

Brian Selhurst looked up at his son as if he'd been betrayed. He'd expected wholehearted support. He'd never known his son to speak against him at a chapel meeting before. The meeting was silent again. The sobbing outside had stopped.

Geoff Notes was bewildered. The Commission had ordered that the chapel should be 'down by Friday' whatever this meeting decided. He hadn't the heart to tell them, however, that all their complaining was in vain. He was stuck for words, and the silence seemed interminable.

At last Alan Drifford stood up and ambled forward. 'Mr Chairman, may I lead the meeting in prayer?'

Geoff's heart sank. He was snookered. To deny the steward an opportunity to pray would be insensitive. He was afraid that Drifford would use the prayer to enlist the Almighty's vote on the side of chapel preservation. But he couldn't think of a valid reason to forbid it.

'Let us pray,' Alan Drifford said, his eyes tightly closed and his hands clasped together. 'Dear Lord, as the senior steward of Gospel End, I am truly sorry. Sorry that I've spent so much of my life worrying about buildings, instead of serving you. I'm sorry, Lord, that I've not prayed enough, or tried to hear your word of guidance. I'm sorry that I've tried to hold on to the past, instead of asking you to show me the way ahead. Forgive me, Lord, that I've held up your work ... instead of helping it forward.' Tears were rolling down from his tightly closed eyes, down the ashen cheeks, and dripping from his chin.

Geoff was now standing beside him, his arm around Alan Drifford's shoulder. 'Yes, dear heavenly Father,' Geoff continued, 'forgive me too. I've been so insensitive since I came to Gospel End, and Lord, I am sorry. Bless my brother Alan, and grant him the wisdom to help lead this fellowship into a new beginning ... that all of us might be your people, for this time.'

The atmosphere was electric. It was one of those moments in church life when you don't talk of the presence of God, you experience it. The issues that seemed so big a moment before were somehow overshadowed by the greater purposes of the Creator.

Steve Jenkins was not a particularly spiritual man but he knew that Alan Drifford's prayer was real. That morning he had glimpsed something greater than Gospel End Wesleyans and spontaneously he stood up and started to sing. He was no singer but the refrain was quickly taken up by all around. It was the hymn of the Wesleyans, a hymn they sang at all the great gatherings of their national conference, and at all the great turning

points in their church's life. It was a hymn by
Charles Wesley.

> Captain of Israel's host, and Guide
> Of all who seek the land above,
> Beneath thy shadow we abide,
> The cloud of thy protecting love;
> Our strength, thy grace; our rule, thy word;
> Our end, the glory of the Lord.
>
> By thine unerring Spirit led,
> We shall not in the desert stray;
> We shall not full direction need,
> Nor miss our providential way;
> As far from danger as from fear,
> While love, almighty love, is near.

The meeting closed. The decision about the future
of the building had been eclipsed by a greater decision. Everything was unresolved, and yet, mysteri-
ously, fully resolved. The Chapel would be
demolished, but the people of God at Gospel End
Wesleyans were marching on undaunted. Someone greater than Geoff Notes had been in the
Chair that day.

Chapter Eight

Patching Things Up

Stan Menston cleared away the last glasses in the empty snug bar on Monday afternoon. Monday lunch-times were always quiet in the Fox and Hounds. He went to the front door and was just about to close it, when he saw Alan Drifford standing solemnly by the church wall. He was looking up at the tall edifice of Gospel End Wesleyans. Stan crossed the road, and stood beside him.

'Gospel End won't seem the same without it,' Stan wheezed.

'I was just having a last look. This building's been like a good friend to me.' Alan Drifford was near to tears again.

'Why don't you come over for a ...' – in circumstances like this Stan Menston would normally have offered a stiff brandy but he stopped himself just in time – 'a cup of tea, or coffee.'

The two men from different worlds sat in the bay window of the Fox and Hounds and drank tea together. From time to time, when conversation lapsed, they just sat and stared out at the chapel as though they were at the bedside of a dying friend. After one such prolonged silence Stan continued to gaze out of the window as he whispered, 'That was a fine prayer you gave on Sunday. It touched all of us.'

Alan, embarrassed and emotional, also gazed out of the window. 'I've got a lot of regrets, Stan.'

Stan was not a demonstrative person but automatically, without even realising what he was doing, he pushed his chubby, stumpy-fingered hand across the table and gripped Alan Drifford's hand with some force. 'We've all got regrets, Alan. Me included.'

The two men looked at each other for the first time. They were both reliving the same memory, and neither needed to mention it. The angry voices echoed down the twenty years since the last time they'd both been in that bar together.

'Get out of here, you freak ... ' Stan had goaded Alan in the smoke-filled snug that Saturday night. The bar was full, and everyone was laughing. Alan Drifford was a laughing stock at the Fox and Hounds.

Alan Drifford was hysterical. 'You killed Mr Jones, slowly but surely, year in and year out. You killed him, with your beers and spirits ... '

'Get out of my pub, before I throw you out!' Stan put up his fist. Threatening.

'You made a decent man into a drunk. You and your cronies. You ruined his life, Menston.' Alan Drifford had stepped over the mark.

The fist had landed squarely on Alan Drifford's

chin and he staggered backwards out of the bar, to the raucous laughter of many men. 'And good riddance ... ' called Stan Menston as he rubbed his knuckles.

And now the hand that had punched him was holding his hand in friendship. 'I've not been much of a Christian, Stan ... I've been more of a chapel man, and there's a world of difference between the two.'

Stan smiled warmly, and looked deep into Alan Drifford's eyes. 'Well, one thing's for sure, I've not been much of a Christian either ... but it's not too late, is it?'

Alan returned the smile. 'No, Stan. It's not too late.'

Meanwhile, about half a mile away, Geoff Notes was standing nervously on the doorstep of the Miss Fields' residence. He pulled the doorbell which tinkled somewhere within and waited impatiently. This was one visit he would rather have left undone. Miss Field senior opened the door cautiously and, seeing it was the minister, unhooked the safety chain.

'Good afternoon, Miss Field, may I come in?' He was trying to sound cheerful and confident, though he felt neither.

'Yes, please come in. It's quite chilly this afternoon.' She showed him into the drawing room and he sat on a very firm couch, the like of which he'd only ever seen in Victorian photographs. 'I'll just let my sister know that you're here, Mr Notes.' She excused herself, and shut the drawing-room door firmly behind her.

Geoff Notes was left in the drawing room for nearly ten minutes, but there was plenty to look at. A large aspidistra loomed over the couch where he was sitting and the table by the window was filled with a diverse range of cactus plants. The Fields' keen interest in gardening penetrated even this inner sanctum which was used only on special occasions.

A large picture in a golden frame depicted Jesus washing Peter's feet with a group of shadowy figures looking on. It was reminiscent of those Victorian pictures which were once very popular in Sunday schools up and down the land. In a beechwood display case were various pottery figurines, memorial mugs and china bowls which were obviously the crown jewels of the Field household. On the top shelf were a number of small trophies and cups which the sisters had won at the Great Orton Annual Horticultural Fair.

On the beautiful marble mantelpiece in front of him was a line of framed photographs which depicted the various family groupings of this old-established Gospel End tribe. One photograph puzzled him, for it clearly showed the Field sisters standing in front of the Selhurst farmhouse with a very young Mr and Mrs Selhurst between them. The foursome had their arms linked together. The two attractive looking Field girls were both dressed in the uniform of the Women's Land Army.

And then he looked at the huge harmonium in the corner of the room and its two manuals of ivory keys which had grown yellow with the years. On the harmonium was a copy of the famous hymn book *Sankey's Sacred Songs and Solos*, which Geoff hadn't seen since his childhood. Geoff checked his watch against the huge grandfather clock. It chimed three-thirty, and was precisely correct. The steady tick irritated him.

At last the door swung open and a tea trolley rattled in, rapidly followed by Miss Field senior and then, rather hesitantly, Miss Field junior. The squeaking trolley was covered with an ornate lace cloth, which when removed, revealed a china tea service with steaming teapot and a plate of warm buttered scones. Once everyone was seated and had balanced their linen napkin, china plate, teacup, and saucer, conversation could begin.

Geoff knew that they would have to work through a mutually accepted agenda of niceties before they could really communicate, and he played the game with charm and patience. They talked about the room, the display of Field 'crown jewels', the weather, their health, his health, his wife's health, and the health of those they all knew in common.

'Another cup of tea, Mr Notes? It is so chilly out there this afternoon,' asked Miss Field senior.

Geoff Notes was running out of patience. 'No, thank you. I, er, I really popped round to see how you both were ... after Sunday morning. I mean, I gather you were rather upset ...'

The two sisters looked at each other. They had already rehearsed their reply. 'No, we're both fine now, thank you,' replied the senior of the two. Field junior smiled and nodded in agreement.

'We've actually written you a little letter, but as

you're here, you may as well have it now, it'll save the postage. You can use the stamp again, if you wish.'

Geoff tore open the expensive white envelope and unfolded the beautiful sheet of bonded notepaper with their address embossed at the top. 'Dear Mr Notes, We have decided to resign our membership at Gospel End Wesleyans. We have enjoyed our many years of fellowship at the church, but feel that it is now right for us to hand over to younger people. We will be attending the Great Orton Methodist Church from this time onwards. With kind regards ... '

Geoff Notes felt sad. He hadn't meant to hurt them. 'Is there any chance that you might change your mind, ladies? The future days at Gospel End are full of hope, and I think we could all be part of something which God wants to do here. Besides, I think your friends at Gospel End will be very disappointed.'

The large grandfather clock chimed four. 'Are you sure you wouldn't like another cup of tea, Mr Notes? There's plenty in the pot,' smiled Miss Field senior.

'No, thank you.' Geoff excused himself. This was a lost cause, and there was nothing more to say. He stood on the step in the chilly November air, and heard the safety chain slide back behind him. Life at the Field household could continue relatively undisturbed.

There was no way that life at the Selhurst farm could continue undisturbed. The news heralded by the *Great Orton Courier* could change a pattern of life which had continued for generations. Brian Selhurst was in a filthy mood, and he knew it. Nothing and nobody was right. No wonder his wife and son had avoided him all day. But now it was supper time, and all three were seated silently round the kitchen table and were tucking into a ham salad. Mr Selhurst was engrossed in the folded newspaper on the table in front of him. Every few minutes Mrs Selhurst would carve several more slices of ham and pile it onto their plates. There was no conversation among them and they were all alone in their thoughts. Somewhere in the background a quiz show crackled on the radio. It filled the silence.

The knock at the door startled all of them. Visitors to the farm were rare enough, and hardly anyone had ever dared to travel that farmyard track across the fields after dark. Mrs Selhurst opened the door.

'Oh, Jenny ... come in, love. It's so cold out there.' Jenny Drifford, immaculately dressed as ever, took off her light brown jacket and handed it to the older woman. She flushed with embarrassment, for she didn't really know why she'd come.

Brian grunted some kind of greeting and looked up from his newspaper for only a moment. John pulled up a chair beside his own and guided Jenny onto it. He felt ashamed of his work-clothes; he'd have changed if he'd known Jenny was coming.

Mrs Selhurst was the kind of hostess who doesn't ask what the guest wants to eat but who loads their plates with everything while assuring them, 'You can leave what you don't want.' Within minutes

Jenny Drifford was struggling to eat a very large ham salad, though of course she refused to eat the ham. A large slice of currant cake and a plate of cheese and biscuits were soon to follow.

'It's lovely to see you, Jenny. You've not been here for years. We don't get enough visitors, these days ... not like we used to. And how's your mum and dad?' Mrs Selhurst was as generous with her welcome as she was with her food.

Jenny soon relaxed. She didn't need a reason for coming because Mrs Selhurst and her son were pleased to see her and the conversation flowed easily between them. Brian, meanwhile, continued to read his newspaper. After nearly an hour Mrs Selhurst brewed another pot of tea and Jenny looked thoughtfully at Brian Selhurst. She suspected that he had already read his newspaper several times and was really listening to the conversation ... wanting to be let in, but not knowing how.

'Is there anything we can do to help, Mr Selhurst?' Jenny asked. Brian Selhurst was startled. He looked up from his paper, his pretence of disinterest gone. He sighed, folded the paper, and dropped it to the floor.

'No, Jenny,' he said sadly, 'I don't think there's anything anyone can do.'

'It's the new town plan, you see,' John interjected. 'It wipes our farm land off the map. We don't want to live in the middle of an estate like that. We're farmers.'

'I hope you don't mind, but I phoned a few colleagues in our company today, and I've got some addresses of people who may be able to help. You might find that in this situation, your best allies are my friends in the Green movement ... '

'Thank you, Jenny. That was most thoughtful of you,' chirped Mrs Selhurst as she held out another mug of tea.

'Yes, Jenny. I doubt if it'll do any good, but thanks, it's nice to know you care.' The crusty expression on Mr Selhurst's face was visibly melting.

'I'm sorry if I upset you at the meeting yesterday,' Jenny continued, feeling that now the time was right for what she had to say. 'I didn't realise how important the chapel building was ... it must be like losing a friend.'

'Everything's so different, Jenny. Maybe I'm just getting old.' Jenny looked into the old man's eyes, and she hoped that, given time, he would come round. These difficult days could yet be a turning-point in his relationship with Geoff Notes.

Nothing more was said, but they all stood up, and Jenny hugged the elderly couple and then buttoned her coat. John walked Jenny slowly over the cobbled farmyard towards her car. 'Thanks for coming,' he muttered, 'it meant a lot.' For some moments they held each other very tight.

The following morning the demolition team invaded the peace of Gospel End. McMurphy and partners had a long-standing arrangement with Head Office to undertake all of the denomination's 'urgent' demolition work. They were able to demolish buildings in a fraction of the time of most other companies in their field.

Unlike most companies they did not wait to prise

out stained-glass windows, haul out pews for resale to the antique trade, or mess around with church organ removals. Their motto was simple: 'Down – and out.' They didn't even worry about removing the hard-core because they knew that local builders would remove it once the word got round. McMurphy's was strictly a demolish and run company. To that end they used explosives.

All day on Wednesday the site supervisor, who was a Scotsman with a degree in structural engineering, clambered over Gospel End Chapel with a paint brush and a tape measure. He was calculating where to place each charge to produce the maximum desired effect. By five pm he had marked twenty-six points in the building where the charges were to be laid and calculated that the explosives should be ignited in five different waves with each wave bringing down a key supporting wall within the structure.

News of the impending demolition spread rapidly around Gospel End all day on Thursday, and soon everyone knew that the great event was timed to occur at mid-day on Friday.

By mid-day on Friday the local police had coned off a wide area around the chapel, and McMurphy's men had nailed boarding over the windows of the Fox and Hounds, just in case of accident. All morning the reporter and photographer of the *Great Orton Courier* were much in evidence.

Geoff and Sarah Notes and a cluster of their congregation stood behind the neat line of traffic cones to witness the great event. There was an air of unreality about the whole enterprise, and

Geoffrey Notes found it hard to believe that Gospel End Wesleyans would soon be down.

The control panel for the explosives had been set up in the rear of the control van, a vehicle specially adapted for the purpose. The three white-coated McMurphy men more resembled a group of hospital consultants than demolition men. McMurphy's had obviously moved with the times.

The senior engineer stepped over the traffic cones and approached Geoff Notes in the growing crowd. 'We wondered if, as it's your church, vicar, you'd like to have the honour of pressing the buttons.'

Geoff beamed. This was one experience that he was delighted to share. It was bound to come in handy as a sermon illustration! 'Delighted ... just show me what to do.'

The senior engineer led Geoff Notes to the 'McMurphy Control Unit', a pristine white van with a long side window and a tangle of cables emanating from it. The rear door was opened and Geoff climbed in and surveyed the buzz of electronic equipment in front of him. There were three swivel chairs, and he was shown to the central one.

The nervous young minister sat on the chair in the back of the demolition unit and posed for a variety of photographs for the *Great Orton Courier*. He then made a brief statement to Sally Finn, the young reporter, about 'this important moment'. The interview over, he instinctively surveyed the chapel for one last time and then gazed at the buttons arrayed in front of him.

The countdown began, and Geoff placed his finger above the first button. 'Three ... two ... one ... *fire*.' Geoff pressed the button, and instantaneously the roof of Gospel End Wesleyans collapsed into the building in a shower of dust.

In all, Geoffrey Notes pressed four buttons, and four times the clouds of dust lifted to reveal another section gone, until at last, only the large facade and doorway remained, silhouetted against the sky like a great cliff.

Just as the countdown for the fifth and final explosion began, the rear door of the McMurphy van swung open, revealing a breathless and bright red Mr Smythe, the planning executive. His eyes were bulging in fury. 'What the hell do you think you're doing? I've got a temporary Preservation Order on this place!'

Geoff's finger touched the last button. 'Touch that, and I'll see you in court!' screamed the pin-striped figure. Geoff lifted his finger. Perhaps he'd demolished enough for one day.

Chapter Nine

A Bad Week

Mr Smythe, the pin-striped planning executive of Great Orton Metropolitan Council, was a skilful politician. He hadn't risen to leadership within the borough so much by his efficiency as by a well-honed ability to take any situation and use it to his own ends.

He walked slowly back to his car with Sally Finn, the reporter from the *Courier*, hovering half a pace behind him. She was asking for 'a reaction' to the demolition, or rather, partial demolition of Gospel End Wesleyans. Even as he walked, his mind was racing around the possibilities which this moment afforded him. His deepest fear about the new town at Gospel End had been 'media reaction', for he feared that local opposition to the new town had the potential to explode into a major national news story.

The public relations course in media management which he had recently completed had

117

prepared him well for this moment. 'Issue trans-
ferral' the lecturer had said, 'can be your greatest
weapon. Preclude the media strike by choosing the
ground you want to fight on. Make sure that you
create the agenda for conflict, not the press. Use
conflict situations to draw the public gaze away
from sensitive and delicate issues.'

'Get in, Sally,' he said brusquely, and the young
reporter obediently climbed aboard Mr Smythe's
gleaming blue Range Rover and looked hopefully
into his reddened face. Both doors slammed shut.
'Now, Sally, what are your contacts like with the
nationals?'

'Okay,' she said, looking rather puzzled, 'but I'm
really better connected with television. I live with
one of the reporters from Regional TV news.'

'Well, you can sell this story how you like, but I
want it sold as widely and as quickly as you can do
it. I'll handle everything from the Council end. I'll
line up as many angry officials as you can use ... but
this Notes man has destroyed the heart of our new
town plan ... and I want him nailed.'

He smiled warmly at the wide-eyed young reporter and hoped that she would buy the suggestion.
If the story she wrote featured a public outcry
about the demolition of Gospel End Wesleyans, it
could successfully camouflage any public outcry
about the building of the new town.

He needn't have worried, for Sally Finn swallowed the bait hook, line and sinker. She couldn't
normally get a Council official to make a statement
about anything, let alone one with any acrimony,
but this time it had been handed to her on a plate.

This local scandal had all the makings of a major human interest story.

Although Sally Finn was only a humble young member of the press community she had full access to the 'club'. She knew that when good stories are fed in, contacts shared, and pieces written, they are notched up in an invisible account of goodwill which can be drawn on later. She might also benefit financially.

She also knew that a major news story could push her career forward rapidly, and she'd always dreamed of getting her name on a by-line in the nationals. Although she was not an ambitious person she recognised that the demise of Gospel End Wesleyans was her moment to hit the big time.

Sally sat in her humble mini and used her mobile phone more extensively than ever before. She dialled through her list of contacts with amazing speed, feeding suitable headlines to whet the appetites of her colleagues on the nationals, and hoped beyond hope that this might be her moment of glory. She spoke of 'Public outcry as vicar demolishes church', 'Town plan dynamited by new vicar', and 'Council outrage at vicar's explosion'.

Time and again the invisible voices replied, 'Thanks, Sally, I owe you one.' Her credit balance in the mystical world of the media had grown astronomically. She had provided the answer to a Friday evening news drought.

Her list completed, Sally ambled over to the grocery store to talk to Mrs Field, her local contact, whose ear was always firmly to the ground. Ten minutes later she left triumphantly armed with the addresses of the Field sisters and Brian Selhurst. She felt sure that she had found three locals who would be willing to speak about Mr Notes' 'lack of consultation', 'undue haste' and 'lack of local support'. From every angle, this was becoming a strong story.

Mr Smythe's media plot worked like a dream, and within hours Gospel End was the focus of a media circus. An electronic television 'news-gathering-unit' scrambled over the rubble of Gospel End Wesleyans, cameras flashed in the milking shed at Brian Selhurst's farm, and a hastily organised 'press conference' in the Council chamber at Great Orton resembled a White House media briefing.

Geoff Notes, the young innocent abroad in this media circus, had never given a press interview before, let alone faced some of the sharpest minds of the tabloid industry. He sat on his sofa and talked naively of 'new beginnings', a 'church building which had outlived its usefulness' and the possibility of 'a new era for Gospel End Wesleyans' without even realising that he was being set up as the villain of the piece.

The reporters all seemed so friendly as they munched Sarah's carrot cake. They were polite and charming, and seemed supportive of his ideas and sympathetic about the structural problems which the church had faced. But behind the smiles and pleasantries and warm appreciation of Sarah's Cambodian coffee they were forming a story which was to portray Geoffrey Notes as the bungling parson who ruined the new town plan and alienated his flock. Indeed, they had him nailed.

The story broke in the six thirty pm regional TV programme *Yorkshire Folk*; a full five-minute feature which included acrimonious interviews with the Field sisters and a very disgruntled Brian Selhurst speaking in his milking parlour. These interviews were interspersed with photographs of what the chapel had looked like before the demolition, and the *Courier* photograph of Geoffrey Notes pressing the buttons in the McMurphy van. The prolonged interview with Geoff had been edited down to a thirty-second statement in which he said the demolition represented a 'new beginning' for the church. The screen then cut to shots of rubble and a sarcastic young reporter saying ' ... but this half-demolished building doesn't look like much of a new beginning to the people of Gospel End.'

Geoff Notes pressed his TV remote-control button and the screen faded to black. His eyes were red with tears. He was lying on the sofa with his head cradled in Sarah's arms, and she was softly stroking his hair. 'What have I done, Sarah? How could I have been so stupid?'

She smiled. 'You've done nothing wrong, love. You've just been set up. But God can even use something as awful as this ... if you'll let him.' When Geoff and Sarah prayed together it was usually quite a formal and predictable routine, but now she gently stroked his hair and whispered: 'Dear Father, we turn to you for help, because there seems no other place to go. We feel so alone, and so unsupported. But, Lord, you haven't left us, and we offer all these problems to you ... please guide us, and even as the world laughs at us ... help us to go on loving in your strength.' There was no 'Amen' to this prayer, but she bent over and gently kissed his forehead.

The snug at the Fox and Hounds was silent as the regulars stood mesmerised in front of the large television screen. As the bulletin ended they paused and waited for Stan Menston to give the verdict. But he could barely speak because he was so upset.

'They've set him up good and proper ... and if I ever hear a word against him in this bar there'll be trouble.' The regulars grunted in agreement. After all, Geoff was the hero of their darts team.

Brian Selhurst was standing in his hall dialling the manse number. His wife was beside him, her eyes ablaze with anger. Brian Selhurst never had liked talking to answering machines, but this was one occasion when he thanked God for them.

'Er ... Mr Notes? It's Brian Selhurst ... I just phoned up to apologise ... I really shouldn't have talked to them reporters ... I was just so angry ... I'll be seeing you then.' It was a one way conversation, and he was glad when it was over.

The Field sisters were seated in front of their television drinking tea from china cups, a ritual which they repeated each evening at about this time. Neither of them spoke, and the television filled the silence. They continued to watch all evening, but they did not speak or even look at one another. An uneasy feeling of regret, which they couldn't begin to articulate, filled the air.

And out in the darkness of the November

evening, just over the road from the Fox and Hounds, a shadowy figure was standing on tiptoe in front of the last remaining wall of Gospel End Wesleyans. An outstretched arm, paint-brush in hand, was daubing in dripping whitewash: 'Praise God! The church lives on!' It was the handiwork of one Alan Drifford, who was enjoying himself more than he could ever remember.

Jenny Drifford was entertaining John Selhurst to tea, and they'd watched the broadcast as they ate hot buttered scones in the cosy lounge of her cottage. There was a wry smile on John Selhurst's face because the interview with his father in the cowshed was quite the funniest thing he'd ever seen on television ... but Jenny was not amused.

'Get your coat on, John,' she said firmly. 'We're going to the manse. They'll need friends at a time like this.'

Jenny rang the doorbell at the manse, but for some considerable time no one answered, so she rang again. At long last Sarah slid off the sofa and ambled to the door. 'I'm busy, and not to be disturbed,' Geoff grunted.

A few seconds later John and Jenny were seated on the floor opposite Geoff, their coats still buttoned. Jenny began, 'We just came to say you did the right thing, Geoff, and we're behind you.'

There was a long pause before Geoff muttered 'Thanks.' He couldn't ever remember feeling so depressed. A few minutes later amid the awkward silence, the doorbell rang again. It was Alan Drifford, his hands and coat splattered with whitewash.

Sarah ushered him in, and he sat on the easy

chair with his daughter at his feet. 'I just had to come to say thanks, Geoff ... I feel like a new man. All my life I've been worrying about that building ... and now it feels like a great burden's been lifted off my back.'

Geoff leaned forward: there was a new joy in Alan's face which he'd never seen there before. 'But, Alan,' Geoff sighed, 'the media have made us a laughing stock.'

'I know,' smiled Alan Drifford patiently, 'but that's not really very important ... not in God's terms. What's important is that Gospel End Wesleyans is no longer a building ... we can become a fellowship again.'

'He's right, Geoff,' Sarah smiled. 'In God's terms today isn't a defeat, but a victory.'

The doorbell rang again and Stan Menston strode in, wheezing heavily. 'The lads at the Fox and Hounds have sent me,' he spluttered. 'They want you to have this.' He handed over a bottle of vintage wine.

In a matter of seconds Sarah had handed out the glasses and Stan Menston had uncorked the expensive nectar. 'To the future of Gospel End Wesleyans ... and what a great future it's going to be,' he wheezed. They all drank deep. Alan Drifford felt that this was one occasion when even a good Methodist could sample forbidden fruit.

And so, slowly at first, the conversation began to flow. They took off their coats and began to relax with one another as never before. Alan Drifford confessed to having vandalised the chapel wall with all the pride of a cheeky schoolboy, and they all began to laugh. But it wasn't hollow laughter, it was the laughter of relief ... of acquaintances becoming friends ... and the laughter of healing. There was a lot of laughter that evening as, one by one, they began to share their own perceptions of what had happened over the last few weeks.

John Selhurst reminded them of the way he'd dropped the potatoes in the 'famine' half of Jenny's display, and Sarah told him how rude she used to think he was. Stan talked of his first trip to church in twenty years, and the shower of plaster during the singing of 'All good gifts around us are sent from heaven above ...'. Alan told them how he and Stan hadn't spoken to each other for twenty years since the night of the fight and how, in the pub the other afternoon, they'd found each other again. Geoff told them how disappointed he'd been that first night at the welcome meeting, but that he'd gradually come to love them all ... and how Alan Drifford's prayer at the church meeting had been the most beautiful prayer he'd ever heard.

Sarah explained the loneliness she'd felt, and described how in her emptiness she'd reached out to Jenny and the Green movement for some kind of support. She was beginning to feel that maybe Geoff needed a good steak and chips ... and Geoff beamed in eager anticipation. Jenny said that before she'd met Sarah she'd practically given up on church, and almost lost her faith. In their friendship, however, she'd caught a new sense of what being a Christian really means.

And as the hours ticked by and the stories

flowed, it was as if, for the very first time, this most unlikely group of people were discovering what it meant to care for one another. For, underlying each story, each glance, each smile, was a growing affection and a deepening sense of trust.

Just how they moved from conversation to prayer wasn't obvious, but it was Stan Menston who, still wheezing, got up from his seat and knelt in the centre of the room and beckoned the five others to join him. And so they knelt in a tight circle of belonging and gripped each other's hands.

'Dear Heavenly Father,' Stan wheezed nervously, 'we thank you that you've taken the chapel building from us ... and we ask you to start again with us as a church. I, for one, thank you for Geoff ... and ask that you'll take this pain away from him. Amen.' The others echoed the amen, and Geoff Notes fought back fresh tears.

The prayers flowed on; prayers of repentance, prayers of hope, and prayers for one another. Geoff buried his head in his hands and sobbed. A few minutes later they were all weeping openly.

It was as if the very presence of God filled the room. What began as tears of sorrow were gradually transformed into tears of joy. There in the circle Geoff Notes felt a healing wave of love flooding over him. This peculiar mix of people stood and hugged each other, and the power of God's love worked a new work in Gospel End Wesleyans that night. The Church of Christ was reborn.

They put on their coats again, and thanked each other for the fellowship. None of them would ever be quite the same again. The pain that Geoff had felt had already gone, and Sarah saw a new sense of hope shining in his eyes.

'Before I go,' Alan Drifford announced, 'I really ought to tell you that Mrs Jones has remembered the chapel in her will ... to the tune of £40,000. But don't get too excited ... there are plenty of strings attached!' And they all laughed together.

There's nothing like a good news story to set the corridors of church power in London humming with panic. By ten am the following morning the 'Central Committee' had gathered to work out their response to the 'Scandal of Gospel End'. The story filled reams of newsprint and was accompanied by various pictures of Geoffrey Notes in the McMurphy van, and the partially demolished chapel.

There was no doubt about it that the 'Central Committee' enjoyed a good crisis. They all knew well enough that to try to make a defence of Geoffrey Notes, or to attempt to explain what had really happened to the chapel's structure didn't have much news value. No, the only viable course of action was to capitulate.

The press officer cleared his throat. 'Well, gentlemen, I think we have the final statement now.' His voice became more formal as he read the committee's verdict. 'Press Release: the Central Committee of the church met today to review the demolition of Gospel End Wesleyans. They concluded that the Reverend Geoffrey Notes had acted hastily and without proper consultation, and that he should be removed from Gospel End as soon as possible. The Central Committee regrets the partial demolition of the church, and hopes that a solution may be found in consultation with the local planning authorities.'

The statement was immediately faxed to a long list of news-gathering agencies, but Geoffrey Notes was already yesterday's news, and this was just another church press release for the bin. The Central Committee retired for coffee. Geoff Notes had indeed been nailed.

The letter from the Central Committee was fairly cold and unfortunately they were unable to find a compassionate form of words to convey their awful verdict. Geoff was seated at his desk with his study as cluttered and messy as ever when he opened the crisp white envelope and read its shattering contents.

'Dear Mr Notes, The Central Committee met in emergency session this morning to discuss the media reaction to the demolition of Gospel End Wesleyans. Your handling of the media during this sensitive operation has left a great deal to be desired, and we are faced with a major national scandal. We have concluded that in the best interests of all concerned, it will be necessary for you to move to another appointment at the end of the year, in a few weeks' time. We trust that you will refer all future press enquiries to the media office. Yours faithfully ... '

The letter was signed by a veritable *Who's Who* of nationally known officials. Geoff's mind reeled as he took in the implications of what he'd just read. As he sank to his knees, he knew he was at the end of his own resources.

'Father, I give you my life, my ministry and my all. I don't care any more about what others think of me ... I just want to be completely yours.' And as he prayed, he saw a picture of Jesus walking up the streets of a big new town. He knew that Jesus had been let out of the chapel at last.

Chapter Ten

The End Times

The media ridicule which made Geoffrey Notes a laughing stock up and down the land did not adversely affect his position at Gospel End. In fact it did quite the reverse: the whole community seemed to gather round him affectionately like a warm cloak.

Geoffrey Notes was seen as the man ready to take on Great Orton Planning Department and as such he was regarded as something of a local hero. He noticed that when he walked down the street people called 'Hello Geoff', and even when he was driving along they waved and smiled.

Their affection also flowed in practical ways and he began to discover a bag of potatoes or a bunch of flowers left anonymously on the manse doorstep. He felt a kind of belonging to this place that he'd never experienced in London. He knew that he would never forget it.

Sarah, too, was beginning to feel more at

home. The music group was meeting regularly at the manse each Friday evening, and there were now eight of them. Every other Monday another group of young people crammed into the manse lounge to learn some new songs and she saw that they had the potential to become a choir of some excellence. They first met just two days after the demolition of the old chapel, but the demise of the building wasn't even a talking point among them. They did not mourn its passing. It was nearly midnight before they had all gone, and Geoff and Sarah were left alone to wash up the coffee cups in the manse kitchen. Sarah was exhausted, yet too excited to think of sleep.

'That was a great night,' said Sarah. 'Those kids can really sing.'

'I know,' said Geoff, solemnly.

'I think they'll make a great youth choir. Three of them are Grade Eight musicians, Geoff ... they know far more about music than I do.'

Geoff nodded, and half smiled.

'I was asking them if any of them had ever done any drama, or dance, because I think we should begin to move into the other arts too. Worship could be such a rich experience for those kids ...'

Geoff pulled the last coffee mug out of the water and dried his hands. He looked lovingly at her pretty face, so alive and so happy. 'Haven't you forgotten something?'

She paused from her drying up, puzzled.

'Sarah, we're leaving here in just under four weeks. There's no way that we can continue with all this ... I think we're getting too involved.'

A flush of anger rose in Sarah's cheeks. 'Who do they think they are, these anonymous men in grey suits who decide where we'll live and when we'll leave? What do they know about us, or what the Lord is doing here?'

'Come on, Sarah,' he said firmly, 'you knew the deal ... during my probationary period I am at the church's disposal. We went into this with our eyes wide open.'

'What a stupid waste,' she said angrily, 'even to think of taking us away from here just when we're on the verge of a real breakthrough. If we leave here now, it's all been pointless.'

'Maybe God brought us here to prepare these people to serve the new town ... or maybe he brought us here to teach us a few things.'

'Or maybe his plan's been screwed up by some jumped up little committee which hasn't a clue about what's really going on, or what the Lord's will is in all this.'

This was one difference of opinion which wasn't to be resolved with a fond embrace and a gentle kiss. It was a difference of opinion which would, perhaps, linger with them for ever.

The following Sunday morning was cold and dark, but a good number gathered at Gospel End School for morning worship. Some came to support the chapel folk during their days of crisis, others came because they wanted to support Geoffrey Notes the local hero, and some came because they really needed the support themselves – and they figured that the Lord might just provide it.

Everyone seemed to enjoy the accompaniment

provided by Sarah's worship band and the enthusiasm generated by the youth choir was quite infectious. Never in the history of Gospel End had hymn singing gone with such a swing.

Geoff had become aware that some members of the congregation were getting weary with the *Freely, freely* books and so had spent a considerable amount of his quarterly stipend on the purchase of an overhead projector. 'This machine,' he assured the congregation, 'will enable us to update our repertoire of new songs each week.' Some members of the congregation seemed somewhat more enthusiastic about this prospect than others.

Steve Jenkins, who had a mechanical turn of mind, was designated 'OHP operator'. Unfortunately, his experience of OHP projection was very limited and the new songs were projected onto the wall in a variety of different ways ... out of focus, upside down, and back to front. To make things worse, neither Geoff nor Steve had realised that there were two songs which started with the word 'Majesty', and the congregation struggled to make the projected words fit a tune for which they were evidently not suited. The song was half sung, or rather not sung, before the whole congregation collapsed into uncontrollable laughter. Such hilarity would never have been allowed in the old chapel. Geoff smiled. He knew that a congregation which can laugh at itself can realistically be described as a 'fellowship'.

There was no laughter during Geoff's sermon, however. As it was the first Sunday in Advent he had chosen to preach on the theme of the 'End

Times'. There was such an earnestness in his voice and such passion in his delivery, that no one could fail to be gripped by his message.

Geoff turned to his text and walked up to the front row of the congregation as he read, 'When did we ever see you a stranger and welcome you in our homes ... The King will reply, "I tell you, whenever you did this for one of the least important of these brothers of mine, you did it for me!" '

Geoff shut his Bible and placed it firmly on the communion table. 'My friends, Gospel End will soon be full of strangers. People coming from all over the country – indeed, all over the world – to live with us here. This will give us a wonderful new opportunity for being present among them, for serving, for caring, and for sharing. We must welcome every new stranger as we would welcome Jesus himself. And we will not reach these people by huddling in our church committees or by locking ourselves behind closed doors. We will reach them by making real relationships with them, one by one. And this church won't grow suddenly – or dramatically – but when you share effective witness individually.'

This wasn't a sermon from a book, it was a message from the heart. This wasn't a nicely calculated theological equation, but the sharing of a vision. The sermon ended with a dramatic announcement. 'Sadly, however,' he concluded, 'I won't be here to join with you in making these new disciples, for Head Office has decided that I am to be stationed elsewhere after Christmas.'

There was a gasp of disbelief from all around the

congregation. Loud whispering broke out among both lines of chairs, and people looked at one another in astonishment.

Instantly Stan Menston was on his feet. 'Don't worry, Geoff, we'll fight them. They can't station you somewhere else – we need you here!' There was a widespread murmur of approval, and someone shouted 'Petition!' Geoff called them to order.

'Please let me continue. Just because Head Office feels that my services are needed more elsewhere please don't get angry or start a petition ... that won't help anyone. Perhaps the Lord brought Sarah and me here to prepare you for the new opportunities which await you, and perhaps our work is now done. Or perhaps he brought me here to teach *me* a thing or two. Whatever the reason, it's his kingdom we're building ... not our own.' He drew his sermon to a close and announced the great Advent hymn:

> There's a light upon the mountains and the day is at the spring,
> When our eyes shall see the beauty and the glory of the King;
> Weary was our heart with waiting, and the night-watch seemed so long;
> But his triumph day is breaking, and we hail it with a song ...

As he sang, Geoff looked hopefully at Sarah, but she was far away in her thoughts. She could see no 'triumph day', only the futility of having to move from a place she was growing to love.

It took nearly an hour for the congregation to

depart. There was much to talk about, and they stood in groups chatting loudly as Mr and Mrs Drifford distributed coffee among them all. But all this time a face kept looking through the schoolroom windows from the yard outside, and it bore a fierce expression. It was Bill Mann, the school caretaker.

At last the congregation departed and Geoff was left all alone to pile the *Freely, freelies* into an old cardboard box. Suddenly the hall door burst open and Bill marched in.

'Well, you've really blown it this time, Mr Notes.' There was a hint of glee in his voice. 'It's nearly one o'clock ... and this is the third week in succession you've gone past twelve. So now I must formally give you two weeks' notice. You'll be holding your meetings elsewhere from Christmas.'

Bill turned and marched back out with a huge bunch of keys rattling by his side as he went. Geoff concluded that Bill had missed his true vocation in life. He seemed to have a natural aptitude for being a jailer.

The young minister slumped into one of the chairs and whispered, 'God knows where we go from here.' He wasn't sure whether he was complaining or praying – but deep down he felt that God would sort it out.

Sarah and Jenny had a lot to talk about after church that Sunday morning. Over coffee Mrs Frederickson had told them that they had been nominated by the Gospel End Residents'

Association to liaise with the Council about the new town plan. Their Action Group had evidently identified them as suitable defenders of the Green Belt against Great Orton Metropolitan Council.

At their first meeting at two pm on Wednesday 4th December they entered the Great Orton Council offices like two frightened schoolgirls. They received the same charming treatment from Mr Smythe that Geoff had received on his visit to the planning office. The percolated coffee, the comfortable seats around the oak table, and the opportunity to peruse the new town plan. But within a few minutes Sarah found herself speaking with a conviction and authority that surprised her. All her hundreds of hours of research into Green issues during her early weeks at Gospel End were crystallising into a coherent argument for a genuinely 'ecologically friendly' new conurbation.

She asked Mr Smythe about the new underpass system for pedestrians which he was proposing; and argued that it was a disgrace to send people underground for the sake of 'convenient traffic flow'. She asked about cycle tracks, and argued that the vast acres of car park were environmentally unsound. And all the time, she was drawing her various proposals with a thick blue felt-tip pen onto his neat white plan.

Within half an hour Mr Smythe was stuttering in embarrassment as he had to admit that he'd never even considered the possibility of a 'rapid tram transportation system'. He seemed blithely unaware of the new transport systems which the Japanese were building into their new towns. He'd never stopped to ask what kind of town the new Japanese residents might be looking for.

He flushed a bright red as Jenny quoted verbatim from the government's latest white paper on 'the provision of green spaces in new towns' and pointed out that his town plan fell far short of the new government guidelines.

Courteously but firmly, he drew the meeting to a close, but was not allowed to do so until Sarah had detailed her proposals for the future of the remaining wall of Gospel End Wesleyan Chapel.

He had expected two country yokels to drink his coffee and grunt approvingly to his neat town plan ... not two young environmentalists with a fuller understanding of current government policy than he had, and a desire to spoil everything with their thick blue felt-tip pen.

At five pm Sarah and Jenny descended the large central staircase with the confidence and assurance of two suffragettes.

'Phew, I'm glad that's over,' smiled Jenny as they walked past the Nissen huts to the car park. 'I really wasn't looking forward to that at all.'

'Me, too,' said Sarah. 'You know, I got the distinct impression that Mr Smythe was scared of us.'

'Well, his lips did quiver when you happened to mention that your husband was the Reverend Geoffrey Notes ... perhaps he feels a bit guilty about something!' They laughed uncontrollably. It had been a good afternoon for both of them.

'One thing's for sure,' said Sarah. 'He really didn't like it when you insisted that people should come first ... not cars.'

At last Jenny and Sarah had a real crusade to fight. There had been something very vague about their previous Green debates, but here was something they could really get their teeth into. Their contribution could actually make a difference. This issue was local, immediate and vital. On their way back to Gospel End they decided to call an urgent meeting of the 'Save the World' Action Group, but it would be renamed the 'Save Gospel End' group.

The changes to the new town plan which they had suggested to Mr Smythe were drastic and far reaching. They would result in Gospel End becoming one of the few new towns which people would actually enjoy living in!

Back in his office Mr Smythe paced the floor. He had evidently underestimated the intellectual capacity of Sarah Notes and Jenny Drifford and his pristine new town plan was now looking battle-scarred from the blue felt-tip lines which these two ecological enthusiasts had drawn all over it.

Mr Smythe did not baulk at all their suggestions – some of their arguments made sound economic sense as well as being environmentally friendly. They had proposed, for instance, that the remaining wall of Gospel End Wesleyans be retained for posterity as a symbol of what the church had once been. The remainder of the site would be cleared and converted into a beautiful garden ... the green heart of the new conurbation. Perhaps this would work better than his previous idea – and perhaps he hadn't been as conscious of the 'greening' of Gospel End as he should have been.

That same evening there was a home match for the Fox and Hounds darts team. Geoff Notes, happy to have escaped from church business, was throwing well. The babble of excitement in the bar grew as the match closed with no victor, and Stan Menston declared authoritatively that there was to be a nail-biting tie-breaker. Minutes later a hush of expectancy filled the air as Geoff threw the final round of the match ... a much-needed double!

The men of the Fox and Hounds jumped up and down and spilled beer everywhere ... and Alan Drifford, who was attending his first-ever darts match, shouted a rather embarrassing 'Hallelujah'. Stan looked across the bar at him and beamed a warm smile, the like of which his regulars had never seen. Then Stan solemnly took the Great Orton Metropolitan Darts trophy, held it high above his head, and shouted, 'We've got it! We've got it!'

After the free drinks had been consumed and the visiting team had departed, the general euphoria began to subside. It was just before closing time when Stan Menston cleared his throat and warned everyone that he was about to make an important announcement.

'Friends,' he began, 'we are all greatly indebted to the Rev Geoffrey Notes for his support, and I'm sure you've all been most disappointed to hear that he is to leave us shortly. I heard today that Geoff has had a spot of bother over at the school, and the chapel has nowhere to hold its services. As owner landlord of the Fox and Hounds, I have decided to let the chapel folk use our old function room in the back yard ... but it's going to need a lot of work doing ... and it's going to need doing before Christmas.' He turned to Alan Drifford. This was obviously a prearranged cue.

Alan took up the story. 'As the executor of Mrs Jones' will, I am instructed to spend the money on a project to encourage temperance in the town. I therefore propose to pay for this refurbishment out of her estate, and for the installation of an alcohol-free lounge bar which can be used for chapel meetings and services whenever required.'

Alan Drifford had ingeniously found a way of supporting the chapel while advocating temperance – and Stan Menston had found a way of using his function room for the sale of soft drinks to a new set of customers. Geoff Notes was open-mouthed in astonishment, for he'd known nothing of the plan before it went 'public'. Instinctively, he knew it felt right.

Whenever Stan Menston asked for help, he could always count on a huge reservoir of goodwill among his regulars. The men at the Fox and

Hounds weren't chapel men, but they were public spirited, and many of them had an affection for the chapel which went back to their childhood days at Gospel End Sunday school. Stan Menston knew instantly that he could count on the support of his men, and he also knew that, whenever they turned their hands to something, they did a fine job.

The rapid transformation of the disused function room behind the Fox and Hounds into a worship centre cum bar was a remarkable feat. The regulars arrived straight from work each evening and laboured until the early hours sawing, plastering, rewiring and plumbing, a pattern that continued throughout the dark December evenings, right up to Christmas.

They were accompanied by a large team of chapel women who were sewing curtains, painting walls and re-upholstering the beautiful oak pub seats which had gathered dust for so long. Geoff was lost for words as he stood and watched the chapel women and the pub men, working together at last.

The morning after the victorious darts match Alan Drifford went down to the chapel and removed his whitewash graffiti. He felt that he'd made his point and that the time was ripe for new beginnings. He spent several hours clambering over the rubble of the old chapel, and picking out pieces of timber which could be used in the new room. He was looking to the future with growing excitement.

Exhausted by his morning's efforts he slowly

collected his last barrow-load of splintered wood. As he did so he lifted a large plank from the rubble and discovered, to his amazement, a large glass container covered in dirt. He dusted it down, prised open the sealed lid with a stick and removed a pile of old faded papers. And as he stood amid the rubble of the old chapel, he read ...

To whom it may concern.

This bottle was buried this Christmas day 1796, on the occasion of the stone-laying of Gospel End Wesleyans.

This congregation began in the stables at the rear of the Fox and Hounds in 1766 following a visit by John Wesley and the outbreak of revival among us. Now, because of the growth of numbers among us, we dedicate this chapel to the glory of God, and we dedicate ourselves to live out this verse:

'Let your light so shine before men, so that they will see your good works, and glorify your Father which is in heaven.' Matt 5:16

Alan Drifford pushed the papers into his overall pocket and ran to show his treasure to Stan at the Fox and Hounds. History, it seemed, had turned full circle.

Chapter Eleven

One Plus One

Gospel End looked like a Christmas card that bright and sunny Christmas Day morning. The roads and houses were covered with snow, and as there had been little traffic through the village the pure white effect remained untarnished.

All was silent as Geoff Notes trudged through the snow in his wellington boots. He walked past Field's grocery store, and the last remaining wall of Gospel End Wesleyans and into the side entrance beside the Fox and Hounds which was clearly signposted 'The Christian Centre'.

He opened the door of the newly converted function room and stamped his boots on the 'welcome' mat, leaving a pile of snow in his wake. He removed his boots, put on his shoes, and smoothed down his tweed suit trousers which had been tucked inside his socks. He stood, just for a moment, and smiled as he surveyed the beautiful new bar cum worship centre. Its pastel colours were a joy to the eye. He had wondered if the room would ever be finished by Christmas, but here it was, smelling of new paint and ready for its first service.

He took the Advent Ring, which had been left on a seat at the back of the room, and paused in quiet reflection as he placed it on the communion table. Then he sat in the front row of the semi-circle of chairs and bowed his head in prayer.

'Father,' he prayed softly 'this is my last day as minister at Gospel End, and I give it to you. You gave this work to me, and now you have taken it away. Help me to accept your will, even when I can't fully understand it.'

As he sat praying he was unaware that Brian Selhurst had entered the little sanctuary and was standing – as ruddy faced as ever – at the back of the church. Brian's hands were stuck firmly in his brown mac pockets, his peaked cloth cap pulled firmly on his head. He was carrying a large plastic bag in his hand. This was his first visit to the new chapel.

For some time he stood motionless until at last Geoff turned to face him. 'Oh, hello, Brian ... I didn't know you'd arrived, I'm sorry.'

'I thought I'd come to chapel today, seeing as it's Christmas,' he said, almost begrudgingly. 'It's not too bad, is it?' He gazed around at the newly refurbished function room. This was fine praise from one whose heart was still in the old building.

'No, it's not too bad,' admitted Geoff, wishing that Brian could have found something a little more positive to say. He tried to be friendly. 'I was glad to hear that the Council will let you keep hold of half the farm.'

'Ay,' said the old farmer, looking suddenly disgruntled, 'I suppose it's better than nothing, but I'll not be bothering about it. I'm handing it over to John. He says he can make more money by going organic. The wife and I are moving into a cottage in the village.'

'And will we be seeing more of you at chapel again, Brian? We've missed you these last few weeks.'

'No, I don't think so,' he murmured. 'The wife and I have joined up at the Great Orton Methodist with the Field sisters. Things haven't changed there, and we all fit in. We all go back a long way together, you know. Anyway, I've brought this for the new place.'

Brian fished around in the plastic bag and took out a large framed photograph of the exterior of the old Gospel End Wesleyans. Nailed to the wooden frame was a small plaque with the inscription, 'This was the chapel where divine worship was held by the Wesleyans 1796–1991.'

'I thought it would look nice on the communion table,' Brian said. 'I made the frame myself.'

'Thanks, Brian,' smiled Geoff. 'I'll put it on the communion table beside the crib.'

He took the frame from Brian's hand and turned towards the table, wishing that he could put this awful picture somewhere else ... like in the gentleman's cloakroom or under the kitchen sink. The photograph did nothing for him except make him feel pleased that the old place was gone.

Nevertheless he was overjoyed that at last Brian Selhurst had returned to worship for the first time since the demolition.

Brian Selhurst took a seat and began to flick through his copy of *Freely, freely*, as if trying to find a song which he knew. Within a few minutes the function room was full of other locals who were all stamping their feet and wishing each other happy Christmas. Several folk even hugged one another and kissed, a very different approach from Christian greetings in the old building.

Stan Menston and Molly marched in with over twenty of their regulars, some of whom had partaken of large whiskies to prepare themselves for the first service in the chapel which they had built together.

Chapel-going isn't easy, especially if you've not been for twenty or thirty years, and some of Stan's regulars were a bit merry. Stan had them well under control, however, and a straight glance from him brought any reveller quickly back into line. By eleven am the new chapel was full to capacity, and it was a matter of standing room only for the latecomers.

The service was a mix of the traditional and the contemporary. They sang 'Once in Royal David's City', but it was followed by a very beautiful calypso-style solo by one of the young people who was accompanied on flute, violin and guitar. The musicians all swayed a lot, but not always in the same direction and some of Stan's regulars clapped along, but not all to the same rhythm. No one seemed to mind.

The drama which Sarah's group had prepared revolved around the phrase 'No room at the inn'. The scene was the Bethlehem Hilton, and it starred John Selhurst as the hotel manager. He was able to find rooms for a whole host of important people like King Herod, the Emperor Augustus and the High Priest.

It was obvious to the packed congregation that he took great pleasure in consigning Mary, played by Jenny Drifford with a cushion stuffed up her jumper, to the garage at the back of his hotel. Seeing her in that condition caused him some amusement but he somehow managed to subdue his laughter by concentrating on his thick Israeli accent. Unfortunately it seemed to acquire a guttural German pronunciation – 'Vot do ya vont me to do abart it, ve are vull.'

The children sang 'Away in a manger', and the youth choir gave a lovely unaccompanied rendition of 'Silent Night'. Other readings followed; but by far the most revolutionary aspect of the proceedings was Sarah Notes' interpretive dance of the Magnificat to a popular piece of electronic music which had recently topped the national pop charts.

Her silky dress and shawl swirled round and round as she twirled in ever decreasing circles, until at last she lay motionless in a crumpled heap on the floor. Geoff Notes took time to explain what the dance meant, in case anyone missed some of the finer nuances of her interpretation. Everyone seemed most impressed, especially the regulars from the Fox and Hounds, who applauded loudly.

Alan Drifford read the New Testament story

about the angels' appearance to the shepherds, and the 'Good News of great joy' which was theirs. He read it with firmness and conviction, raising the volume of his voice when reading words which he felt were of particular theological importance. It made the fine tuning of hearing aids extremely difficult.

Geoff had timed the lighting of the Advent Ring to coincide with this reading so that it provided a visual focus. He lit the four large red candles around the holly ring during the early verses of Luke's Gospel Chapter 2, but when Alan reached the angel's speech he shouted, 'This very day in David's town your Saviour was born – Christ the Lord,' and Geoff lit the large central white candle.

Brian Selhurst could take no more. The drama, the dance, the music – it had all been different enough, but the sight of five candles on the communion table was more than he could bear. He jumped to his feet.

'Mr Notes, I must protest. All these candles. It's nothing short of popery. Mr Wesley must be turning in his grave, it's not Wesleyan to have candles in a chapel.'

Before he knew what he was doing he was out at the front and blowing out the candles. Geoff was devastated. This was his last service, and the dedication of the new church – what was more, it was Christmas Day! He'd planned to leave a happy and united fellowship looking to the future, but now it seemed hopeless. Why did this have to happen now?

John Selhurst, now fully composed again,

stepped forward. 'It's Christmas, and we've come to worship Christ our Saviour. If the candles upset people, let's leave them out ... but nevertheless, let's carry on ... after all, it's his day.'

'Thank you, John,' said Geoff, still winded.

Jenny Drifford stepped forward. 'Yes, let's carry on ... but with the central candle alight. For Jesus said "I am the light of the world."' Without another word she ostentatiously relit the central candle and glared at Brian Selhurst, as if daring him to make a counter-attack. He remained rooted to his chair. The congregation was silent and tense.

Geoff abandoned the sermon he'd prepared, for he saw what had just happened as a symbol of his ministry at Gospel End.

'This week, Alan Drifford discovered this dusty bottle in the rubble of the old chapel.' Geoff held the bottle high, and read its contents. The congregation gasped in delight, and sensed a great continuity with the past as they realised that Gospel End Wesleyans had met behind the Fox and Hounds before, long ago.

Geoff paused for effect, aware that every eye was on him. 'On Christmas Day, almost two hundred years ago, the Wesleyans remembered the Light of Christ entering the world, and committed themselves to be lights at Gospel End. Today, as we look at this lighted candle, I invite you to take up the commitment of your forefathers, and to shine for Jesus at Gospel End. Will you pray for another person and tell them about Jesus so that the church can grow, one plus one?'

Geoff took the central candle and slowly relit the

other four, and as he did so, he said, 'Let your light so shine before people, so that they will see the good things you do and praise your Father in heaven.'

There were no tears. Geoff didn't want there to be. It was Christmas Day ... a time for joy, and hope and new beginnings. The perfect day for moving on to pastures new ... and for leaving his friends to their new-found mission.

The service ended, and the air filled with a loud buzz of conversation as the people from Gospel End each bade their farewells to Geoff and Sarah Notes. Nice things were said, and genuinely meant, but Geoff did not enjoy farewells, and he longed for the ordeal to be over. Sarah was fighting back tears, but they were not tears of sadness: they were tears of anger. Of course she would follow her husband to 'pastures new' ... but more out of duty than out of conviction. To her, the church authorities had really screwed things up, and she and Geoff had to pay the price.

After the coffee and hot mince pies the assembled congregation was brought to order by Alan Drifford.

'Geoff and Sarah, thank you so much for coming to Gospel End. We have learned so much from you – and we promise to go out in the Lord's strength to grow God's kingdom here, as you put it, 'one plus one'. Now, as the last act of Geoff's ministry here, let's go and bury the bottle again.'

They donned their coats and wellington boots and trudged in procession behind Geoff and Sarah to the remaining rubble behind the old building.

Quite naturally, it seemed, they formed a semi-circle round the deep hole which Alan Drifford had prepared.

Geoffrey Notes cleared his throat. 'My friends, as minister of Gospel End I have prepared a short note to be buried in the time capsule along with the other things.'

Standing in the deep snow, in the stillness of that Christmas morning, the people of Gospel End surveyed their young minister for the last time. He stood, confident and erect, gazing round at them as if he were about to read his last will and testament. In a real sense, it was just that.

To whom it may concern.

This bottle was reburied on Christmas Day 1991, on the occasion of the opening of the new Christian Centre behind the Fox and Hounds.

The congregation used to gather on this site, but, sadly, our building and our traditions became our first love. Now, because of the outbreak of revival among us, we dedicate this land to the people of Gospel End, and ourselves to the sharing of the good news about Jesus with all who will come to live in our town.

Matt 5:16 – 'Let your light so shine before people, so that they will see the good things you do and praise your Father in heaven.'

In ink, beneath the typewritten note, Geoff hastily scrawled the simple insignia 'One plus One', and the black outline of a candle burning bright. The paper was folded and inserted into the old glass bottle.

In a flash of inspiration, Geoff invited Brian Selhurst to bury the time capsule, a task he willingly undertook. As the oldest surviving member of Gospel End Wesleyans it was his rightful place to conserve the past for the future. Slowly and ponderously Brian took the bottle, and then handed it on to his son, John. 'It's over to you, now, lad.'

The strapping young farmer knelt in the cold wet snow and gently laid the time capsule in the hole. The members of Gospel End Wesleyans applauded, and as soon as John was on his feet again Alan Drifford shovelled the earth over the bottle. Slowly, the little crowd went their separate ways for Christmas dinner, and Geoff put his arm round Sarah's shoulder as they trudged silently home. Their work at Gospel End was done.

Geoff stamped his boots on the concrete path in front of the manse while Sarah turned the key and pushed the heavy front door open. The phone was ringing, and she dashed to the study to reach it just in time.

It was Janet in Shetland. 'Happy Christmas,' she said. 'I felt so lonely I just had to phone you. How are you guys?'

'We're on the move again,' sighed Sarah. 'They're sending us to Inner London next week.'

'Wow, that's great news,' said Janet enthusiastically. 'It's what you always wanted!'

'Not any more,' answered Sarah. 'Now we want to stay here.'

'Well I never,' Janet replied, 'after all you said about Gospel End, I can't believe it!'

'By the way,' Sarah concluded, looking at what lay on the cluttered desk in front of her, 'did I ever thank you for that candle?'

Epilogue

The old glass container lay hidden in the dark earth undisturbed across the years while above, the cold winds of change blew across the little community of Gospel End. It lay there for fifty years, silent and entombed, like a seed waiting for springtime.

This bottle was more than a cluster of memorabilia. It was a freeze-frame of time, and it contained the hopes of a young minister called Geoffrey Notes, long dead and long forgotten.

At last, the long wait was over, and the still silence of the darkness was broken by the scraping of a shovel. Eager hands reached into the darkness, and the ancient glass container was pulled out into daylight. Old, wrinkled hands brushed the dirt away, and prised the lid open.

They were the hands of Jenny Selhurst, formerly Jenny Drifford, now an old woman, and all alone again. Her husband John was dead and her three children had all left home. She stood there as a single woman again, as she'd been that Christmas Day so many lifetimes ago.

Her mind filled with pictures of the way that things had looked before Geoff and Sarah had left: the old village still intact, and the new town only a dream on a council plan. Things had been so different then.

She looked up, and all around her, in Wesley Park, she saw the excited faces of many friends. Black faces and yellow faces, old faces and young ... hundreds of Christians crowding in to catch a glimpse of the treasure in the old woman's hands.

And as she held the bottle in her hands, and gazed out misty-eyed over all those excited faces she thought she saw – leaning forward in anticipation – the faces of Geoff and Sarah, Brian, Stan and Molly and Mrs Jones ... and then, just for a moment, the face of John, so handsome and strong, that Christmas morning so long ago.

Someone held a microphone to her lips. 'My friends,' she said, 'I stood on this spot on Christmas Day fifty years ago today and watched this bottle as it was buried in the soil. I would like to read you the letter which our minister, the Rev Geoffrey Notes, wrote that day ... his last day as minister in Gospel End.'

She carefully handed the bottle to a friend, and pulled out the tarnished brown paper and unfolded it. But it was blank ... Geoff's typewritten message gone for ever. But beneath, in bold black ink were the three words she spoke

for all to hear ...

'It simply says, "One plus One" ... and the sign of a lighted candle ...'